THE HOUSE THAT CRACK BUILT   1

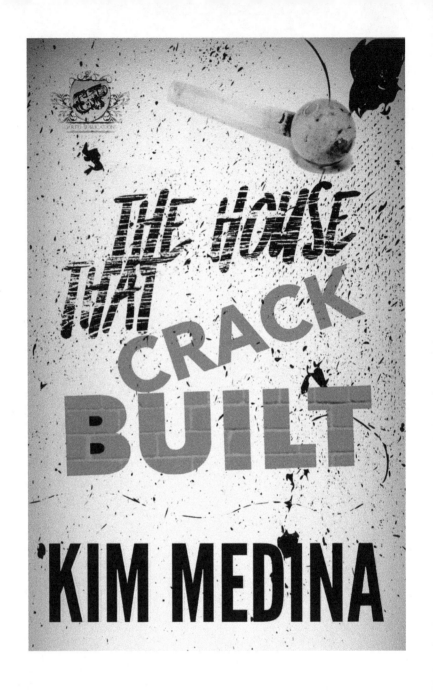

THE HOUSE THAT CRACK BUILT

By KIM MEDINA

ARE YOU ON OUR EMAIL LIST?

SIGN UP ON OUR WEBSITE

www.thecartelpublications.com

OR TEXT THE WORD: CARTELBOOKS TO 22828

FOR PRIZES, CONTESTS, ETC.

CHECK OUT OTHER TITLES BY THE CARTEL PUBLICATIONS

4

By KIM MEDINA

WWW.THECARTELPUBLICATIONS.COM

THE HOUSE THAT CRACK BUILT   5

THE HOUSE THAT CRACK BUILT

BUILT

BY

KIM MEDINA

Library of Congress Control Number: 2017955523

ISBN 10: 1945240245

ISBN 13: 978-1945240249

Cover Design: Cover Design: Bookslutgirl.com

www.thecartelpublications.com
First Edition
Printed in the United States of America

What's Up Fam,

This year is rolling right on by. I can't believe we're almost through September! Before I jump into anything, we would like give our love to all the people that were effected by Hurricane's Harvey & Irma. We are truly praying for you and your families during this time.

We have begun production on *Bmore Chicks* – Season 2 and are very excited about it! If you haven't already done so, slide on over to YouTube and check out Season 1, also available in DVD.

Now, on to the book in hand, "The House That Crack Built". I absolutely LOVED reading this tale. It has all the things I look for in a great book, and is full of drama and suspense. I'm positive you'll love it too!

With that being said, keeping in line with tradition, we want to give respect to a vet or trailblazer paving the way. In this novel, we would like to recognize:

TARAJI P. HENSON

Ms. Taraji P. Henson is hands down one of my favorite actresses. She can currently be seen on the FOX TV show, "Empire" portraying Cookie Lyon. For her work, Ms. Henson has received a Golden Globe, been nominated repeatedly for an Emmy and in 2009

By KIM MEDINA

was nominated for an Academy Award. Recently, she penned her first novel, *Around The Way Girl.* It's a memoir about her life, family, friends and the grinding it took for her to leave Washington DC and go to Hollywood with a dream. We couldn't be more proud of Taraji at Cartel Publications so make sure you take some time and check her novel out!

Aight, get to it. I'll catch you in the next book.

Be Easy!

Charisse "C. Wash" Washington

Vice President

The Cartel Publications

www.thecartelpublications.com

www.facebook.com/publishercwash

Instagram: publishercwash

www.twitter.com/cartelbooks

www.facebook.com/cartelpublications

Follow us on Instagram: Cartelpublications

#CartelPublications

#UrbanFiction

#PrayForCeCe

#TarajiPHenson

CARTEL URBAN CINEMA'S 3rd WEB SERIES

BMORE CHICKS
@ Pink Crystal Inn

NOW AVAILABLE:

Via

YOUTUBE

Don't Want To Wait? Purchase the ENTIRE
Season via DVD Today!
(Season 2 Coming in December)

www.youtube.com/user/tstyles74
www.cartelurbancinema.com
www.thecartelpublications.com

By KIM MEDINA

CARTEL URBAN CINEMA's **2nd** MOVIE

MOTHER MONSTER

The movie based off the book,

"RAUNCHY"

by

T. Styles

Now Available on You Tube

Available to Download via VIMEO

www.cartelurbancinema.com and

www.thecartelpublications.com

CARTEL URBAN CINEMA'S 2nd WEB SERIES

IT'LL COST YOU (Twisted Tales Season One)

NOW AVAILABLE:

YOUTUBE / STREAMING / DVD

www.youtube.com/user/tstyles74

www.cartelurbancinema.com

www.thecartelpublications.com

By KIM MEDINA

CARTEL URBAN CINEMA'S 1st WEB SERIES

THE WORST OF US (Season One & Season Two)

NOW AVAILABLE:
YOUTUBE / STREAMING/ DVD

www.youtube.com/user/tstyles74
www.cartelurbancinema.com
www.thecartelpublications.com

CARTEL URBAN CINEMA'S 1st MOVIE

PITBULLS IN A SKIRT – THE MOVIE

www.cartelurbancinema.com and
www.amazon.com
www.thecartelpublications.com

By KIM MEDINA

#TheHouseThatCrackBuilt

"Houses, like people, bring with them the sins

of the past.

You have been warned."

By KIM MEDINA

THE HOUSE THAT CRACK BUILT 17

PROLOGUE

The walls were angry. Splattered with blood, vomit, sweat and mold, the house was dead along time ago, its existence fit for nothing but a blazing fire that would hopefully set it free. And yet broken bodies, carrying diseased and addicted minds roamed around the place hoping that one hit of crack, just one, would relieve them of the wretched space they found themselves in.

A woman, her gut filled with a nine-month-old fetus sat crouched in the corner, her legs wide open, a pipe pressed against her lips, exceeded in getting herself high. She ignored the obvious, that she was in labor, warm amniotic fluid flowing under her body.

And then someone had done it.

A lit match from a broken window was thrown inside, its flame following the gasoline trail that was placed for it earlier that day. Jolted with the juice of fear, the only chemical more powerful than drugs, the addicts went flying out of the house to keep what was left of their lives.

As the fire grew stronger it appeared evident that no one would occupy the premises again.

By KIM MEDINA

But all who thought this would be wrong.

CHAPTER ONE
AMINA

Why we always gotta eat dinner at the table? I think my mother only does it because it was her way of controlling us. And then she got a nerve not to be ready so we can eat.

Me and my brother Drillo was waiting on my mother, who was still on the phone with the rental office as they made excuses on why they couldn't do what she asked, meanwhile my sister was out in the streets probably being a whore.

"Toni, I need that van out of here!" My mama said placing a plate of fried chicken on the table. Then she scratched her short curly bush. Mama was big but she was pretty when she wasn't trying to get me to do stuff which was all the time. "I already told you I don't know where it came from. But I do know I have kids, and a rape van parked in front of our building that's scaring the hell out of all of us. Every time I walk by it I swear I hear somebody cussing me out. Just move it already!"

Drillo laughed and I hit him.

By KIM MEDINA

"They done already broke the windows." She continued to explain. "What you think I'm doing this for? The last thing I want to do is keep calling about something I asked you to do weeks ago." She placed Lemon Lime punch on the table. "And yesterday Wanda said some kid crawled inside and almost died because it was hot out. Ya'll in for a lawsuit trust me!"

She placed mac and cheese on the table.

"Yeah, whatever, bastard! I'm gonna sue this entire fucking building and I'll play all the phone calls I taped of me asking you to move it too." She hung up.

"Ma, did you really tape the calls?" Drillo asked.

She threw her hand in the air, waving him off. "Amina, go see if your sister is walking up the street."

I frowned. "But I'm hungry."

"Well we ain't eating without her so find out where she is or starve." She threw her hands up in the air. "As mad as I am right now I don't even care."

I smacked my lips and rolled my eyes. "Shoot! She always late and messing stuff up."

I knew I was supposed to walk with my sister to the store earlier and figured she went by herself. Candy and Pepsi's was her best friend and she would do anything for them. Even walk in the darkness I guess.

"Okay, mama."

She placed her hand on her hip. "Amina, what did I do to make your red ass so selfish?"

"I ain't but she—"

"Sometimes I think you forget you're seventeen! For one thing you *wayyyyy* too immature for your age." She paused. "Don't you think you should wanna wait for your sister so we can eat as a family?"

"Okay, mama I'm going already." I rolled my eyes when she wasn't looking.

I opened the door, walked down the steps and pushed open the building door. It was a little cooler than it had been so that was okay I guess. Just like my mama said, the black van, with no tags, was kinda blocking my view so I walked outside and around it to look up and down the block. From where I was standing I saw my boyfriend Jordan's building.

He's a snack and every girl at school couldn't believe that instead of them he wanted me. People

By KIM MEDINA

said he favored Quavo with his small dreads and height but whatever he looked like he was all mine. Plus since we started fucking it made him want me even more.

My sex life I had to keep to myself because mama said if she ever found out I was doing those things, she would send me to Mississippi to live with Auntie Margaret, who looked like a man.

You don't understand, I loved it in D.C. and never wanted to leave. I mean stuff happened all the time around here but stuff happens everywhere right?

I walked a little further down the street when I heard a noise somewhere near.

Since my neighborhood was kinda bad, I moved closer to the door in case they were shooting and I could run inside. Standing in the doorway I heard it again. This time it seemed like the noise was coming from the van, like somebody was moving around inside of it. Maybe fighting.

Fuck that!

I ran upstairs and busted into my apartment. "Mama! Somebody in that van outside!" I pointed at the door. "You gotta call the police like you said!" I walked up to her. "I think they fighting or something."

My mother stomped toward the yellow phone on the wall. "You see...I knew this shit would happen. They probably doing all kinds of stuff in there. Smoking drugs. Drinking! All of it!" After punching the numbers in she said, "Yeah, police, I need somebody to come to my house right now! I think somebody in the van again." She paused and then gave them the address. "I know you don't know what van I'm talking about but it's here anyway."

I walked over to the window and could see that the back door to the van was now open.

"If another kid almost dies in that bitch it'll be on your heads if yah wait too long." She paused. "Because I can tell by the way you talking to me that you don't care." She paused again while I continued to look at the van.

For some reason my heart was pumping hard, like I was watching a scary movie. I heard something when I was outside in the van so that was for real. I didn't know what I was about to see but something told me it wouldn't be good.

And then I did *see something* and turned my head slowly to look at my mother. It was like time

24   *By KIM MEDINA*

stopped. It scared the life out of me. "Ma," I said softly, my voice kinda lost in my throat. "Ma, you gotta come over here."

"Wait a minute, Amina. I'm—"

"Mama, come now!"

She looked at my legs. "Amina, are you..." she covered her lips with her hand. "Are you, peeing on yourself?" Her eyes widened and she dropped the phone and ran toward me. Pushing the curtains aside she looked out the window and saw what I did.

My sister's legs dangling outward, one of her shoes off and sitting on the ground.

CHAPTER TWO

AMINA

I don't think nobody likes hospitals but I hate them the most. I once saw my grandmother die in one. She was talking to me and the next minute her eyes widened and the fluids left her body. It was yellow, like lemonade and I didn't know why. I can never get the thought out of my mind but mama said I should try.

Easier said than done.

After that, the next year I had to stay in one for a month due to really bad pneumonia. I begged everyday for mama to come get me but she never did. I stayed in a room with another person—an old lady who kept farting in the middle of the night and stinking up the place. I didn't have to deal with her long because she died too.

We were in the hallway when the doctor walked up to us. He was a white man with strawberry splotched skin, which looked like it itched real badly. "You can see her now, Mrs. Hartwell."

By KIM MEDINA

Me, mama and my thirteen-year-old brother rushed past him and into her room. She was awake but she didn't look the same. Like she was older now even though she was fourteen.

"Baby, I'm so sorry," mama said kissing her forehead. "That you had to go through all of that." She rubbed her braids backward. "You gonna be fine now, trust me. I'm here and I'm not gonna let anything else happen to you."

The doctor walked into the room. "I'm sorry, but I forgot to tell you that she isn't speaking much." He whispered, moving in closer. "But she'll be okay with a little time. Won't you kiddo?"

Tamika looked away.

"I don't understand, why is she doing this?" Mama asked.

He looked at Drillo and me. "Maybe we should talk in private."

Mama's eyes moved toward Drillo. "You stay in here with your sister so me and Amina can talk to the doctor." She pointed at him.

He frowned. "Why I gotta fucking stay?"

Mama slapped him into the only available seat in the room. "That's why. Need another reason?"

I don't think he did.

When we walked outside the doctor said, "Ma'am, I don't think that was necessary. Hitting a child like—"

"You tell me about my daughter's care." She pointed at him with a stiff finger that seemed to grow the longer she held it out. "And let me tend to my son."

He took a deep breath. "As you know the perpetrator raped and sodomized your child. And although she isn't suffering any major internal damages, only lacerations of the vagina and anus, the mental implications can be far worse and last longer than we can anticipate. To put it bluntly, this is very serious."

Mama placed her hand on her head. Her body was trembling. "So, so what do you think we should do?"

"I have a few ideas. For starters I don't think you should go back to that building." He clasped his hands in front of him. "The psychological damage alone could throw her off even more."

"What do you mean don't go back?" Mama asked. "Are you telling me that we should move? 'Cause I don't know what you think I got, but it sure is not a lot of money. I'm a waitress. I ain't got no—"

"Your daughter will be traumatized further than you realize if you return. And I'm talking beyond measure." He lowered his brows.

I looked over at mama and could tell she was thinking about moving even more now. This was the worst possible situation for my life. I had to stop it right away. "She'll be fine." I said. "I'll let her stay in my room. She always liked it there right, mama? We can play games and stuff. That way—"

"Amina, shut the fuck up!" Mama scratched her bushy curly hair. "Besides, I know what you doing and any decision I make gonna have nothing to do with you."

I stayed quiet but nobody was taking me from my house and my boyfriend. If I moved what was to stop him from getting with another girl? That's why everyday I dreamed of having enough money so that nobody could tell me what to do. If I had money I could tell mama to fuck off and leave me alone.

"Ma'am, I don't know what the move will mean for you and your family, but to me you don't have a choice. Didn't you say they didn't find the man?" He paused. "Whatever you got to do to leave that property I suggest you do. And now."

The motel was the nastiest thing I'd ever seen in my life. And mama was making us live in here like were dogs or something. It had two beds and because Tamika got raped and didn't feel comfortable sleeping with anybody, mama and me got one bed and Drillo had to sleep on the floor on blankets.

When we unpacked our clothes mama went to McDonalds and got us all Happy Meals. We ate them quietly as we looked at one another. I knew we were gonna get on each other's nerves and we hadn't been here long.

Tamika took two bites of fries and went to sleep and mama told Drillo and me to sit on her bed so she could talk to us.

"We gonna have to watch your sister closely," she whispered.

"But what that mean?" Drillo asked.

Normally I despised anything he said but this time I was with him all the way, because I wanted to know too. "Yeah, I'm kinda confused."

"It means that you have to stay with her and see what she needs. Especially while I'm at work."

I frowned. "So we can't go to school either?" I asked.

"Shut up!" Drillo said punching my leg before I slapped him in the back of the head with an opened hand.

"Stop it!" Mama yelled before we started fighting. "Both of you." Tamika opened her eyes a little but closed them again before rolling on her other side, away from us.

I rolled my eyes. "Mama, I can't not go to school. I thought you said education was important."

"Amina, do you hear yourself talking sometimes?" She paused. "You know education is important to me. Don't be stupid!"

"Then I'm confused."

She took a deep breath. "Your sister is suicidal." She whispered. "The doctor told me when you were inside with 'Tamika."

"What that mean?" Drillo asked.

"It means she thinking about taking her own life. Since the man didn't do it himself. And until I find another place for us to live," she paused. "All of us, we staying here and not going back home no time soon."

I got up, opened the door and stomped outside. My mother was ruining my social life and she didn't care. The only thing on her mind it seemed like was my sister who was getting on my nerves. Just 'cause she got raped don't mean I got to suffer.

What about me?

I leaned against the wall and crossed my arms over my chest. Mama walked up to me. "What is wrong with you, Amina?"

"Nothing." I rolled my eyes. "Just leave me alone."

"You know what, it's my fault you so selfish." She paused, before pointing at me. "You were my first born and I had you thinking that you were the only thing in my world that mattered. And when the others were born, I didn't want you having to feel like you were a young mother because that's what my mother did to me, by making me watch my siblings all the time." She moved closer.

"But let me clear things up for you." She continued. "The world out there is cold and it don't mean shit if you don't have a family you love to remind you what life is all about." She pointed at me. "And one day life gonna rain down on you hard, Mrs. Redness. And you gonna remember this moment." She paused and pointed at the door. "Now if my little girl dies because of how you treating her you gonna see a part of me only my enemies know about. And I mean every last word I say."

She stormed away.

CHAPTER THREE

AMINA

I was looking at Tamika who was lying on her side in the motel room. She wasn't crying or doing anything that made me think she was sad so in my opinion she was just doing this to get attention. Like always.

Ever since she left the hospital and we moved into this motel it was the same thing everyday. She would stay quiet, Drillo would go outside and scratch cars and I would look at whatever channel came through on the small TV while mama went to work. When I was super bored, which was every day, the other part of my time would go into trying to call Jordan but he was always too busy to talk.

Mama just dropped off snacks before leaving back out for work and I looked at her. "You want the Doritos?" I asked her. She was looking at me but she wasn't saying anything. "Tamika, you ever gonna talk again?" She blinked a few times but didn't say anything. "You wanna tell me about what happened that night?"

She still wouldn't talk.

By KIM MEDINA

"Are you mad at me for not going with you to the store that night?" She rolled over, with her back in my direction. "This is stupid!" Frustrated I got up and walked toward the door. "I'm leaving."

When I got outside a man was sitting in a black Mercedes. The car was real shiny and stood out from all the mess. He was kinda cute or whatever but way older than me. I wish I had his car though. My cousin April said her boyfriend let her drive his whenever she sucked his dick.

"Damn, sexy, who you in there with?" He asked me.

I smiled. "Nobody. Just my sister and stuff."

He waved me over. "Let me holla at you for a minute." I walked to the car and could feel my ass bouncing as I moved toward him. "Damn you fine."

"Thank you." I said.

I stood next to the window. "You like what you see?" He asked me, smiling real hard.

His car smelled good and his dreads were nice and neat, so I guess he was cool. "Yeah."

"Good, 'cause you cute." He looked me over and then at the motel. "What you doing around here though? You serving?"

"I don't know what that mean." I frowned and scratched my head before smoothing my bun.

He nodded. "Yeah, aight, well get in my car."

I grinned. "Okay."

I rushed around and slid into the passenger seat. The moment I was inside, he winked and put his hand on my thigh. It was warm and turned me on a little.

"I like your hair like that." I smoothed my bun again. I didn't see what was cute about it because mama never gave me money to get my hair permed. Saying I should keep the natural texture. Instead it stayed in a puffball on top of my head. "It makes you look innocent." He touched it. "What you mixed with?"

I shrugged. "Black I guess."

He nodded. "Well you gonna be mines." He ran his thumb over my bottom lip and something said to leave. But wasn't nothing to do in the room. "You like that?" I smiled and nodded again. Felt like that was all I could do for some reason. "You hungry?"

"Kinda."

"Wanna go to Red Lobsters?"

My eyes widened. "You must got a lot of money! 'Cause my mama said only people with money can go there."

"Well your mama's right." He paused. "But before we go I just got one stop to make."

"Okay." Now I was real excited because I was tired of McDonald's food or peanut butter sandwiches.

"I like you." He rubbed my leg and then touched my hand. "You easy going. Not like a lot of these females out here. How old are you again?"

"Seven...I mean eighteen."

He rubbed the tip of my fingers. "Wow. I would've thought you'd be older since you so mature."

"Ahn, ahn, just eighteen." I paused. "But my mama says I'm too immature. I told her I wasn't though. Glad you can see it too."

"Shhhhhh." He placed a finger over my lips. "You talking too much."

I mouthed the word, "Sorry." But it couldn't come out all the way because he was pressing my lips down.

He put my hand on his crotch. "I like how you touch me like this." His eyes grew wider and now

THE HOUSE THAT CRACK BUILT 37

he looked crazy. "You like what you feeling? This right here is all dick. Not like them boys you go to school with. I'm all man."

I didn't like it at all but I didn't know what to do. My heart was beating fast and I wanted to go home but technically I didn't even have a place to live. And then he got real gross and started growing under my hand. His stuff was way bigger than Jordan's and I was scared.

"You want to be nice to me? For taking you out to eat."

"Yeah...kinda."

"Well do me a favor, touch my dick," he said. "The skin part."

"Huh?" I moved back and he pulled me closer. "I...I don't know—"

"You know what I'm talking about!"

He frowned and stuffed my hand into his jeans. His penis felt icky and I wanted to go back to the motel. I was scared and thought he would rape me like my sister got raped. Now I realized it was dumb to get in.

"I'm kinda tired. Can you take me back to the motel?"

"Nah. Fuck that." He yelled. "Now rub that joint. Hard. Like you trying to yank it off." I did what he wanted. He was still driving while his dick was getting so big I thought it would pop out of his jeans. "Keep it like that." He continued while moaning, his tongue hanging out the right side of his mouth. "That feels so good. Mmmmmmmmm."

And then I felt wet stuff all over my fingers and he grew quiet. "Hold up, what the fuck are you doing with your hands in my pants?" He snapped and started being crazy.

"Huh? You told me to." I removed my hand, and this greenish-yellowish stuff was all on my palm. It didn't look like Jordan's and it was gross. I rubbed it on my jeans just to get it off. And now I had a stinky stain on my clothes.

"Whatever, look, I just remembered I got something to do. So we ain't goin' to no Red Lobsters." He pulled over and parked. "You gotta bounce."

I looked around and didn't know where I was. "But can you take me back to the—"

"Yo, get the fuck outta my car before I beat yo ass!" He yelled so loud he spit on me.

I pushed the door open and stood on the curb. He pulled off.

I walked behind my mother as she stomped into the rental office of our complex. It was a few days after I met that creepy dude and I didn't feel like going anywhere. Just staying in the room and eating. But mama said she wasn't about to have two daughters tap out on life so I didn't have a choice.

And no, I didn't tell her what happened. She hadn't beat us in awhile but I'm sure she would.

"How can I help you?" Angie, the meanest leasing agent in the building asked. She wore huge glasses to cover the dark circles under her eyes.

"You know what I want, Angie. Why is my apartment still not ready? The first thing they told me after the van was moved was that it was being fumigated. And now they telling me something wrong with the ceiling. What's going on?"

"What's going on is that you need to wait." She rolled her eyes.

"Angie, it's been weeks. I don't have no money for no motel room and three kids to take care of."

"Pam, I don't make the apartments available, maintenance does. Now just for your information they are fumigating the entire building and that's all the update I have right now. Don't act like we ain't got a bunch of roaches up in this bitch. You know it needs it badly."

"But my family's living in a motel. And I don't see no other families evacuated from the building. It seems like since we called about the van and my daughter being raped, management been trying to cut me off."

"All I can say is you gotta wait."

"But we living in a—"

"PAM, PLEASE! I'm busy!" She yelled. "You ain't the only tenant we have you know."

Mama moved toward the door.

"Pam, I'm sorry about Tamika. I really am."

Mama took a deep breath, turned around and walked out. I followed of course even though I wanted to run away from her I was so embarrassed. Besides, Angie's daughter was one of my friends at school. I can only imagine what people said behind our backs.

When we got outside I looked over at her. "What we gonna do now?"

"Something you won't like." She sighed. "But as you can see, I don't got much choice now do I?"

CHAPTER FOUR

AMINA

I knew something was wrong when she opened the door all happy and stuff. But when she said she was taking us out to eat my heart beat faster in my chest. Mama never took us out to eat unless something was wrong because she claimed she never had money. So what were we doing sitting in T.G.I.Fridays?

"I got some bad news," she said.

"You scaring me, mama," I replied.

"Well I need you strong not scared." She pushed her plate to the side, which held and uneaten hamburger and fries. Me, Drillo and Tamika looked at her strangely. "We leaving DC. Angie called me back and I think we found a house."

My eyes widened. "Please don't say we going to Mississippi, mama. I don't wanna leave my friends and stuff."

"Can I have your fries?" Drillo asked me.

"Just shut up and listen!" She slammed her hand on the top of the table. "Both of you." She took a deep breath and placed her hand calmly on top of Tamika's. Why do we get fussed at while she gets loved? "We can't move back to that apartment right now. I have a lawyer looking into our case about what happened to your sister. And she said it wouldn't be a good idea for safety reasons to go back. And staying away makes our case better. In fact, she says we should never go back."

"I knew this would happen," Drillo laughed. "You owe me five dollars, Amina."

"But you promised it wouldn't be forever, mama!" I yelled. "I don't wanna leave!"

"Amina, it's out of my hands. You were with me the other day. You saw that I tried. But now I'm looking at this as a sign from God. Maybe he doesn't want something else happening to you in that neighborhood."

"So I gotta leave school too?"

"Amina—"

"This is unfair!" I ran out.

By KIM MEDINA

I knew my aunt wouldn't want me at her house when I knocked on the door and I was right. When she opened it a little wider I saw a man sitting on the couch, his pants were half undone. But for whatever reason she let me in anyway.

We were in her bedroom and I was sitting on the edge of the bed as she stood over me with crossed arms over her big titties, which was hard I'm sure 'cause they were huge. "I can't do that, Amina."

"Just for a little while though. I wouldn't have asked if you weren't in my school district."

"Look, my house ain't fit for no kids. Plus if I let you stay, Drillo gonna get mad."

"Why he gonna get mad for?" I frowned.

"He called me and asked ten minutes before you came and I told him no too. Now I'm sorry but the same holds for you." She sighed. "So you gotta leave and I gotta go make my money. He already irritated. Probably getting ready to leave and everything."

"But I need your help! You my aunt. Please! I'm gonna lose everything if she makes me leave D.C."

She flopped next to me. "Amina, you gotta grow the fuck up. Or you will find yourself in a situation you not prepared for."

"You mean be a hoe like you?"

She frowned.

"I'm sorry."

"I know you are," she said. "That's the problem."

"So the answer is no."

"Yes, for the millionth time. YOU CAN'T STAY HERE!" She paused. "Besides, you're only moving to Baltimore. What's the worst that could happen?"

"Stop saying that," my cousin April said to me as she spread a blanket on the floor I would sleep on tonight. "You know you can always stay with me. No need to say thank you."

I sat on the comforter and crossed my legs yoga style. I looked around and tried not to let her see me frown a little. I didn't want to live here because it was nasty, sticky and smelled like

By KIM MEDINA

must but the good part was that my uncle was on drugs and didn't really care about who was in his house, as long as they didn't bother him or bring the cops around.

That was the main reason my mother didn't visit her brother and never wanted us to either. His wife left him a long time ago for her pastor and I think that's when he started using.

"Well thank you anyway 'cause ma tripping." I took off my shoes. "Talking 'bout we gotta move to Baltimore."

She laughed. "You do know that ain't far right?"

My eyebrows rose. "Yes it is! To me! You can't catch Metro there from here. You gotta drive and in case you forgot I don't have a car."

"Girl, shut up with all that nonsense."

"What?" I scratched my scalp.

"At least your mama cares." She held her head down. "I haven't seen mine in two years." She exhaled and looked like she was about to cry. Now I wish I didn't bring it up. "Anyway, I don't wanna talk about all that right now. Whatever happened to that dude in the Benz? Did you see him again?"

"No...and don't tell nobody either." I wiped my hand down my face. "That was so embarrassing."

She waved the air. "Girl, like I know your weak ass friends."

"I'm serious. I don't—"

Someone knocked on the window and I excitedly jumped up to open it. Jordon, my boyfriend, was on the other side. He was wearing a white t-shirt, fresh jeans and new Jordon's. I turned to look at April. "Can you make sure your father don't come in here?"

"He don't care about all that but I got you." She waved at Jordan. "Hey!"

He winked and we sat on the floor. "Why you ain't been answering my calls? I miss you." I kissed him. "And what took you so long to get here?"

"My moms acting stupid as fuck." He shook his head. "But I'm here now so it's whatever."

"I thought you wasn't coming though." I tried to hold his hand but he pulled away. "Is something wrong?"

"Why you here?" He asked with an attitude.

"What you mean?"

"You up in this nasty ass place with your freak ass cousin." He looked around like he hated

By KIM MEDINA

everything. "And then you call me over when you know I'm not feeling it."

"You mad at me or something?"

"Nah."

"That's what it feels like."

"Man, I got some shit on my mind but it ain't nothing you need to be worrying about."

I grabbed his hand and squeezed it softly. "Well you wanna have sex?"

His face softened a little. "In here? On the floor?"

"We did it before."

"Yeah but we were at your house too. We might as well be sleeping outside by the dumpster."

"Jordon, my mother wans us to move to Baltimore and I don't wanna go. I mean, what if I can't see you no more? Can't we stop all this fighting and—"

"Aight," he shrugged. "We can do whatever you want."

We lie down and I pulled the top cover over us so we both could take our clothes off. Then he rolled on top of me with his warm body and pushed my legs apart softly.

"Fuck...," he moaned.

"I love you," I said softly.

"Damn, you feel so good," he replied. "And why you wet already?"

"'Cause I'm thinking about you."

Before I could say anything else, the door opened and April walked inside. "Don't mind me. Yah can finish whatever you was doing. I'm going to bed."

"Should we stop?" He whispered as she straightened the bed before cutting the lights out. Now it was pitch dark.

"No." I smiled. "We don't have to stop."

"Good, 'cause this feeling right."

I opened my legs a little wider. "If I gotta move we still gonna be together right?" I whispered in his ear.

He kept moaning.

"Jordon, if I leave D.C. we still together right?"

CHAPTER FIVE

AMINA

"So you and Jordan look like you was having fun last night," April said as we walked home from school. "Plus I thought yah was gonna go on forever. Must be nice."

"I guess."

I was nervous all day because I thought my mother, who I hadn't spoken too all night and day, would pop up looking for me. And then April said I probably didn't have anything to worry about because she would probably never think I went to school.

Guess she was right.

So why was I sad about it?

"I'm serious," she nudged my arm.

"It was okay but I think something was on his mind." I wiped my hair behind my ear because it was flying in my face. April flat ironed my hair last night and now it reached all the way down my back. I thought Jordan would notice at school but he didn't say anything to me all day.

"He don't seem to like me though." She adjusted the book bag on her back. "It's whatever." She shrugged. "He got a big one?"

"A big what?"

"Dick."

"So you really asking me about my boyfriend's package?"

"You were on my floor," she giggled.

"It's still gross."

She rolled her eyes. "Okay, Amina, it ain't that serious. I was just kicking it with—," April stopped in midsentence. "Hold up, ain't that auntie?"

I followed where she was pointing and saw my mother's blue Honda. "Oh my, God! How did she know I was even here?"

"Well you know I ain't tell her."

"I wish she just leave me alone!"

"I ain't trying to be rude but you gonna have to stay some place else, Amina. My dad stay high and we don't need the police 'round these parts. They probably would find all kinds of stuff in the house. I'm sorry but you gotta go."

I was sitting on Jordan's steps waiting for him to come home. All I knew was that I wasn't moving with my mother to Baltimore, even if I had to stay on the streets. Or friends' houses night to night. The funny part is my mother had zero respect for me so that's why she didn't bother to come to the school. Had she thought just a little about how much it means to me she would've found me. Instead she messed up my situation at my cousin's house.

When Jordan finally came home he was walking with his friends and they were all laughing about something. But he frowned when he saw me and said a few words to them before they all walked away. Like he was seriously irritated he stomped toward me.

"You ain't speak to me at school today." I said. "That really hurt my feelings."

He rolled his eyes. "I ain't gotta speak to you for us to be together." He paused. "Wait, you not here to tell me you pregnant are you? 'Cause I don't need that right now."

"What? No!"

"Then what you doing here?"

I looked around. "I need some place to stay."

"Well you can't stay here. My parents ain't having none of it. Plus they think you too fast anyway."

I frowned. "But they never met me."

He shrugged. "They still think that though."

I scratched my head. "Well did you tell them that I was a freak or something?"

"You can't stay here, Amina," he said ignoring my question. "It ain't even an option."

I sighed. "Well what am I gonna do?"

"What is so bad about Bmore, Amina?" He yelled. "Maybe you should just give it a chance."

"You not there for one. And I...I don't know nobody out there." I felt myself about to cry and tried to stop it because he hated when I acted like a baby.

"Stop all that or I'ma walk away. I'm dead ass." He looked around like he was expecting somebody and back at me. "Plus ain't nothing for you to be crying about anyway. It's just a move. It's not life or death. You always so extra."

"But I'm gonna have to leave, Jordon." I wiped the tears away that crept up on my face anyway. "And I don't want to if you're not there."

He sighed and looked up at the sky. "Like I said you can't stay here but I may know a place you can chill a few days.

I jumped up and hugged him. "Thank you! Thank you! Thank you!"

"Don't thank me yet. I gotta ask first and it may not go down like you want."

We were standing in Dannie, Jordan's play sister's, house. As I looked at all the high tech stuff she had in the living room I couldn't help but feel a little jealous of her life. They had money for nice furniture and stuff and we were in a funky motel.

Her father walked out from the back room, shook Jordan's hand, before kissing Dannie on the back of her shoulder. "Don't forget to take the chicken out." He told her.

"I won't daddy," she said winking at him.

When he left Jordan picked right back up on the conversation. "It'll only be a few days," Jordan said. "Not forever. Just until she figures something out."

I forgot how pretty she was as I stared at her. Her hair ran down her back and her body was on point even though my hair was still longer than hers.

While she listened to him she crossed her arms over her chest. I think they thought they were whispering but I heard every word said. "This is so dumb, Jordan." She said to him and then looked at me. "Just go home, Amina. Your mom will understand why you ran away."

"It's not just that though. I don't wanna move. Plus I been gone overnight so she gonna be mad and probably punish me. If she does that Jordan gonna get salty 'cause I won't be able to see him."

She looked at Jordan and he looked away. I think he was laughing.

Dannie blew a raspberry. "Okay, I guess you can stay for a little while. But every night you gotta leave at 6:00pm and come back thirty minutes later, to pretend you just came over. That way my father won't know you living here."

"I can do that." I smiled.

56 ***By KIM MEDINA***

She looked at Jordan. "I'm doing this for you."

"I know," he kissed her cheek. "That's why I fucks with you." He walked over to me. "Look, I gotta go. She's gonna give you some clothes but stay outta her way too." He pointed in my face. "Don't be filling her head with all that dumb shit you be trying to do me. About our relationship and stuff like that. Keep your thoughts to yourself. This real live putting my friend out."

"I won't mess up, Jordan." I held his hand. "You coming back later right?"

"I'll get up with you when I can." He walked away.

For a week he would come over and fuck me, talk to her privately and leave. Something told me he wanted her but I could never put my finger on it. Plus I was scared to bring it up or I could get thrown out.

The only reason I was fighting going to Baltimore was for him so if he didn't want me I didn't know what I was going to do with my entire life.

I figured I would step to her about their relationship but when I opened the door what I saw threw me off. Her father was sitting on the recliner in his room, his hand on the back of her head while she was on her knees sucking his penis.

I closed the door softly and ran away, not saying a word to either of them.

CHAPTER SIX

AMINA

I waited for Jordan to come out of school because I couldn't wait to tell him that I saw Dannie having sex with her own father. I hadn't been to school in weeks because April told me my mother was looking for me when I called her earlier on the phone. So I had to hide on the side of the building and wait.

I saw Jordan walking out of the building but before I could tell him about Dannie, I saw him coming out holding my cousin April's hand. My heart was pounding and my stomach turned as I rushed toward them. "What you doing?" I yelled at her. "Huh? What you doing?"

She scratched her hair and then her face and I could tell she was nervous. This was probably the real reason she wanted me gone. It had nothing to do with my mother coming over or her father getting high. "I thought you dropped out." She looked around at the people walking past us.

"What you doing with my boyfriend?" Jordan laughed once and turned toward April. "I'll meet you in the car."

I stopped him by standing in front of him. "Jordan, why you treating me like this? You really gonna walk away without saying anything?" Tears rolled down my face.

"What I tell you about acting like a baby?"

"But you cheating on me." I grabbed his hand.

"Get the fuck off me before I drop you." He slapped my hand away.

"I'm never talking to you again! Ever!"

"Ain't nobody checking for that trash pussy anyway." He laughed and walked off.

"Jordan, I—"

My cousin placed her hand in the middle of my chest, stopping me from rushing behind him. "Let him go, Amina. Don't play yourself more than you already have. I mean look around, people watching and you look ridiculous."

"What are you doing with him?" I yelled in her face. "And how long have yah been doing all this?"

"A year."

I stumbled backwards. "So you let me stay...you...you watched us have sex and he was...your boyfriend?"

"Girl, I didn't want it to be like this but he's mine. I even called your mother and told her you were at my house, hoping she would come get you and you would leave, but you didn't." She sighed. "At least now you know you can go to Baltimore 'cause ain't nothing keeping you here."

My stomach felt as if it was about to explode and I held it with my palm. All of a sudden something came over me. I looked at her, grabbed her hair and pulled her down. When she was underneath me I stomped on her face with my grey flip-flops while she was hitting my legs with her fists.

I was kicking her with everything I could and then she bit my ankle. I dropped to the ground and tried to pull her off of me but then she yanked my hair.

That's when I felt something burning on my side. When I touched it the pain grew stronger and when I glanced at my fingers I saw they were covered in blood.

"What did you do?"

April was breathing heavily and she was holding a bloody knife. I tried to crawl away but she stabbed me again, several times in the back and arms.

TWO WEEKS LATER

My mother helped me inside of her car and every part of my body ached. I was in the hospital for two weeks and my mother looked like she aged fifteen years. Before she pulled off she took a deep breath and turned toward me. We haven't spoken about why I ran away but now I think it was coming. "Amina, why did you leave me?"

I rolled my eyes.

"First you were gone two weeks and then you go and get yourself stabbed."

"Don't act like it didn't happen from your niece."

"Amina, we have to keep this family together."

"Mama, I don't feel good." I sighed deeply. "All I wanna do is lie down before—"

"I know you're hurt and I'm sorry. But you don't just run away when things don't go your way. When things get rough that's when you pull for family even more. You scared me, Amina! Don't you see what you've done?"

By KIM MEDINA

"How come you coming down on me when my world is ending?" I paused. "You acting like you don't care about nothing I'm going through. It's all about Tamika these days. I know I'm just a kid mama but my cousin and my boyfriend were together and now I gotta change schools."

"And you'll get a better boyfriend. One who will make you realize how much time you wasted on that fool to begin with. You may even meet him in Baltimore." She paused. "Amina, do you realize your sister cried everyday you were gone?"

"Whatever, mama. She don't even talk."

"That ain't got nothing to do with her eyes. You her sister. Don't you see how your disconnect hurt?" She paused. "Not only her, but you too."

"Mama, can we just go?" I paused. "Pleaseeeeeeeee!"

She exhaled. "Okay, Amina. Okay."

BALTIMORE

Me, my mama, Drillo and Tamika stood in front of a brick house that looked like it would fall over at anytime. Smoke burns were around some windows and I figured somebody tried to set it on fire. I wish they had finished.

The street had trash littered all around and there were small groups of people watching us. Mama said it wasn't Baltimore, but a small city on the outskirts called Reisterstown. And if we walked a few blocks that way we would actually be in Baltimore city.

Now I'm really confused.

All I know was that I was looking at the ugliest house I'd ever seen.

"This looks haunted," Drillo said.

I shoved him even though he was right.

"It's ugly but we can make it home," mama said smiling at it like it was smiling back. "The uglier the vessel the more love it can hold." She looked at us. "Your lives will change for the better here. Wait, you'll see."

Suddenly a car pulled up and a big fat man walked outside of it. He stepped up to my mother and burped before scratching his belly. "Sorry about that. Just left the diner."

My mother frowned. "But Angie told us to be here an hour ago." She looked at her watch. "We been here ever since waiting on you. It's not very professional."

"Well I'm here now." He dug into his pockets and handed her a set of keys. "Now remember the deal we made over the phone." He pointed at her. "You make the repairs on the basement, one of the bedrooms and all of the bathrooms. You do that and the rent is $200 a month and we will look at rent to own options afterwards." He paused. "The two other rooms are ready for beds and most of the house is habitable."

"Most of the house is habitable." She repeated. "What kind of nonsense is that?"

"Look, you getting a deal. And I'm surprised my cousin Angie even called me because she said she didn't like dealing with you at the rental office. Must feel guilty about something if I know that woman." He looked at the house. "Yep, this place has seen a lot but don't worry...she keeps secrets well."

Mama took a deep breath. "I just need a place to hold my kids. I'll worry about my own secrets."

"She'll do that too." He burped again. "Well, I gotta go. They keeping my food warm at the diner."

"Wait...you going back?" Mama asked.

THE HOUSE THAT CRACK BUILT   65

"Hey, I'm a big man. I like to eat." He climbed back in his car. "Remember what I said, make the repairs and stay away from all drama. I get one more citation from the State of Maryland and they condemning this place and I can't have that." He pointed at her. "I'm counting on you and your family."

"Wait, what happened here again?" Mama asked.

He smiled and pulled off.

By KIM MEDINA

CHAPTER SEVEN

AMINA

I was sitting on the porch looking out into the neighborhood when the air suddenly smelled like perfume. It meant my mother walked outside. "How you feeling?"

I rolled my eyes. "Fine." I paused hoping she wouldn't pull me into a long conversation. "Ma, when can I get a cell phone?"

"I'm tired of you asking me for a cell phone." She paused. "You need to be cleaning the stitches because I'm sure they infected by now."

"The stitches are gone, remember? I caught a bus to have them removed last week."

"Oh, that's right." She walked in front of me. "I'm so sorry. My mind has been...been gone lately. So you gonna be mad at me forever?"

"Mama, I don't wanna be here. What else do you want me to say? Or would you prefer if I fake like we cool? All I wanna do is be left alone."

She sighed. "You know what...I'm not doing this. If that's how you feel I'll give you your space for now. I told Drillo he could stay home from school. Maybe he can help you with cleaning the trash out of the basement."

"You mean the syringes?"

"Amina, please!"

"I just wanna be clear that you told Drillo for reasons I don't know, that he can stay and get on my nerves while I clean out trash from a house that should be clean."

"I told him unless he's helping in the basement to stay out your way. Make him and Tamika ham sandwiches for lunch and don't let him run the streets." She looked around. "Peter kind of scared me and I don't know what we facing yet by living over here."

"Okay, mama." I sighed. *Just go.* I thought to myself.

"And give it a chance, Amina. This place may change you for the better." She got in her car, smiled and pulled off.

When I looked up the street I saw the older lady I met when I first got here, removing groceries from her car. I rushed over to see if she needed help. "Want me to take them?"

"I'm fine, honey," she smiled. "I sure am glad a family moved over there. You wouldn't believe the things I've seen come out of that house. Finally maybe this block will have some peace."

Before I could ask her what she meant, Drillo screamed, "Amina, come here!"

When I turned back to talk to Mrs. Connelly she was gone and so were her groceries. That was definitely quick. I walked over to him and asked, "What you want?" I sat down on the porch.

"Nothing. Just calling your name." He's so annoying. And to prove it he sat next to me, his sweaty thigh resting against mine. That meant he did it on purpose.

"Get off me."

He didn't.

"I'm hungry," he said.

"Well I'm not cooking right now."

He got up, nudged me a little. "Well suck my dick, bitch." He ran into the house. Normally I would chase him and punch his back but whatever.

I was about to go inside too, until I saw a white lady and a kid walking quickly in my direction. She was holding a boy's hand who looked to be about eight years old and her hair was matted all over her head. Her pale skin had so many large bumps there was no smooth surface. When she made it to the house she moved closer and walked toward the door to open it without even speaking.

"Can I help you?" I stood up.

"No, I'm going inside." She acted like she didn't have to say a word to me. Or like I wasn't there.

"This is my house. Are you looking for someone else?"

She looked at the house and back at me. "Wait...you bought this place?"

I nodded.

She broke out into laughter and walked away.

"Who are you?" I yelled. She ignored me. "I said who are you?"

"Ain't no need in talking to her," a girl said standing next to me. She had two other girls with her and they all had long braids. One was red, the other blonde and the one talking to me was blue. "She ain't nothing but a zombie."

"But she was trying to get into my house."

She looked at the other girls and they all broke into laughter. What the fuck was so funny in this neighborhood? "And that ain't gonna stop. People feel like they own that house since most of them spent time there." She extended her hand. "The name's Chestnut. What's yours?"

"Amina."

"Hold up, don't you got a cousin name Amina, Yolanda?" She asked the girl with the red hair.

"Sure do," she said popping gum.

"Anyway, yah really gonna move in this house?" Chestnut asked. "'Cause I heard it was supposed to be condemned."

"Yep, my mama said nobody ever gonna live here again," Yolanda said. "And here you are. Yah must be real bold."

"Who you here with?" Chestnut asked.

"My mama, brother and sister. We fixing it up to own it."

"Oh...she like strict or something?"

"Nah...well...kinda. But I still do what I want."

"Yeah right," Yolanda said. "We seventeen, well, Yolanda will be in a few days. How old are you?"

"The same."

"So what makes you think you can do what you want if you the same age as us? Unless your mama don't give a fuck 'bout you either."

"I don't know...but I did run away for some weeks."

"Then why you come back?" The blonde braided girl asked.

"That's Gucci," Chestnut said. "And she don't like nobody so don't mind her."

I stuffed my hands in my pockets. "I came back because I got jumped and stabbed. I fought five girls off." I knew it was a lie but so what. I didn't want them thinking they could mess with me like my cousin.

"Yeah right," Gucci said. "She faking to pump her profile."

I raised my shirt and let them see the patches on my stomach. Still pink because they were kinda fresh.

"Damn," Chestnut said. "You like bad ass or something? Where you from?"

"D.C., Southeast."

A car pulled up all of a sudden. It was a blue BMW with black tinted windows. I don't know how he saw out of them. Seconds later the car windows rolled down and a dude with dark skin and wavy hair appeared. He was wearing really black shades. "What ya'll doing over there?" He asked and for some reason I was scared.

"Nothing," Chestnut said. "Just hanging with Amina."

72   *By KIM MEDINA*

"And who that?" He asked.

They all pointed at me.

"You live over here, girl?"

I nodded yes.

He laughed hard and pulled off.

"Who was that?" I asked.

"Somebody you don't wanna be anywhere near." Yolanda said.

"But she should be okay though since she a girl and—"

"SHUT UP, GUCCI!" Chestnut yelled, hitting her in the arm.

"He lived here or something?" I asked.

They giggled again and the laughing was really starting to irritate me. "Like I said, leave it alone," Chestnut said. "Anyway, we 'bout to get some smoke. Wanna come?"

I looked at them, crossed my arms over my chest and then stuffed my hands in my back pockets again. My mama gave me a lot to do today but if I turned down the first people I met I would never have any friends. "Yeah, I can come by later after I do some stuff here."

She gave me the address, which was in walking distance. "See you later." She pointed at me. "Oh yeah, and I don't like to be stood up so make sure you come. Or you dead to me." She waved and they walked away.

"You can't go with them," my brother said standing behind me in the doorway.

I didn't even know he was there. "Leave me alone."

"Okay, but then I won't tell you what Tamika just did to herself."

I just finished cleaning up Tamika's bedroom because she peed and boo-boo'd all over the middle of the carpet. I don't get what would make her do this. Even though I cleaned it up, the smell wasn't fully out and I had to open the windows to let it air out some. The thing was it was hot out and that made it stink even more. And because she hadn't spoken since she was raped, she didn't tell me why she wanted to be so gross. When I looked over at her she was sitting on the bed quiet.

"What's wrong with you?" I asked. She lie down with her back faced me. "Tamika, why did you do this shit?" I walked up to her. "Talk to me." She didn't open her mouth. "You know what, fuck this and fuck you. I'm out." I walked out and slammed the door behind me."

"That's all the money I got," I said, giving it to my brother. It ended up being five dollars and some change. "Now don't tell mama I left or I'm gonna tell her about that time you stole from 7-Eleven." I pointed at him. "You know how she feel 'bout that kind of stuff. She'll still fuck you up."

"Yeah, aight." He sucked his teeth and stuffed the money in his pocket. "Just don't be out all night."

"How I'm gonna do that? You know she off at 9:00 anyway."

"Well, I might go to the store and—"

"I paid you to stay in the house!" I yelled in his face. "I'll take you to the store tomorrow when ma go to work." I walked toward the door and when I looked back at him he was smiling. "I'm serious!"

CHAPTER EIGHT

AMINA

I was walking down the street to meet Chestnut when I heard some people fighting in an alley, a street up from the house. At least that's what it sounded like. When I looked between two houses I saw two men kicking another on the ground. I was about to scream when someone covered my mouth with their hand and dragged me away.

"You crazy or something?" Some guy asked me. He was taller than me and his braids were neat and thin, running down his back. "Them niggas would've shot your face off. Who are you anyway?" He looked me over. "Why I never seen you 'round here before?"

"I...uh..."

"It don't matter. Just bounce before the cops show up and start asking questions." He paused. "And I'ma say this too because you look kinda green. If they get to asking questions you ain't seen nothing." He jumped in his car and pulled off.

I ran away from the alley and back toward my house. I wasn't interested in going to Chestnut's

By KIM MEDINA

anymore. That idea really went out the window when I saw my mother's car pulling up in front of the house. It was like everything was trying to stop me from going to her crib.

But why?

My mother must've gotten off early and didn't let us know. She must've been trying to pop up on us. Trying to be slick and shit. This woman is gonna ruin my whole existence. Sometimes I wish she was dead.

First day over here and my life was fucked already.

"What you doing out here?" My mother asked when she saw me walking up to her. "You make dinner like I told you because it sure don't look like it?"

"Uh...yeah." I looked behind me again, I was just trying to get to know the neighborhood since you forced us to live here."

"Amina, just stop it." She paused. "Come over here and help me with these bags. I'm tired and don't feel like all the lip flapping right now."

I grabbed one grocery bag and we walked in the house where Drillo was sitting on the sofa watching some porno in the living room.

Everything about this was strange. Why would he do that?

This was not gonna end well at all. This boy is crazy.

"What the?!" Mama yelled before walking up behind him and smacking him in the face before turning off the TV with the remote. "What's wrong with you?"

"I was just..." He pointed at me. "Amina, was about to go see a boy!" To get himself out of trouble he tried to throw me under the bus with a lie.

"What?" Mama yelled.

"No I wasn't!" I looked at her. "I was just gonna...meet some...I mean—"

"You know what, I'm not dealing with this now." She kicked off her shoes. "Where's Tamika?"

When she disappeared in the house looking for my sister I walked up to Drillo. "Give me my money back. You in here acting like a stone cold freak and you lied on me."

"Yeah right!" He laughed. "Suck my dick." Why did he always say that? He walked away and there was a knock at the door.

When I opened it Chestnut was on the other side and she had an attitude. "So you stood us up?" When I looked behind her Gucci and Yolanda were standing with crossed arms over their chests. "I thought you were coming by and—"

"Who is that?" Mama asked.

I slammed the door in Chestnut's face and walked toward my mother before she could see them. "Huh?"

"Who was at the door?"

"Nobody."

She frowned, walked toward me and pushed me to the side. "One day lying gonna catch up with you."

She opened the door and my breath was trapped in my throat. I stood behind her and looked over her shoulder. Luckily I didn't see anyone there. She closed the door and said, "You got school tomorrow. It's an early night. Go to sleep."

I rolled my eyes and went to the bathroom that wasn't all the way finished on the bottom level. I didn't have to go but I just wanted to be alone. Everything about this neighborhood felt wrong and when I tried to fit in by meeting new people and doing new things, my mother ruined it by popping up early. She wanted children who acted like furniture and that wasn't me.

I was about to go into the living room when I heard somebody talking on the side of the house in heavy whispers. I didn't know her for long but I could tell the raspy voice was Chestnut's and I think she was talking about me. "She shut the door in my face."

"I told you that bitch was fake," Yolanda said.

"I told your ass over and over," Gucci said, "No new bitches. When you gonna realize it?"

"Just be quiet," Chestnut said.

"You mad though?" Yolanda asked.

"Never mad over a bird bitch," Chestnut said. "Let's go see what Russo doing."

"Russo? You know he not gonna let us in," Yolanda said. "He told you not to come by his house no more or—"

"I know what he said, bitch," Chestnut snapped. "Let's go."

By KIM MEDINA

I just left my new school and was sitting on my porch when a black pick up truck pulled up on me. When the window rolled down it was the guy who covered my mouth near the alley. He was smoking something with a light on the end that smelled like strawberries. But all I could see at the time was that he was so cute and that was different from when we met at night.

"You okay?" He asked. "I hope I didn't ruin your day."

I stood up, dusted off the back of my jeans. Standing next to his truck I said, "Who are you?"

"We can get into all that later. First, get in."

"For once I'm gonna say no." I said.

He smiled. "So you used to getting in the cars with strangers and now you wanna be brand new on me?" He paused. "Sure it don't have nothing to do with me putting my hand over your mouth?"

"Nope."

"Then what is it?" He sat the lighting thing down.

I liked his smile and was warming up to him even though I didn't know why. I tried to tell myself the same thing happened with the guy in the Benz and that it was obvious I didn't know what was good for me. "Maybe I'm playing hard to get."

"Okay, if that's the way you want it."

He was about to pull off until I yelled, "Wait!"

He stopped. "You getting in?"

I opened the door and slid inside. "Can I have your name?" I asked.

"You hungry?"

"So I'm in your car and you gonna be secretive?" I put my seatbelt on anyway.

"No secrets. We gonna get to know each other." He smiled again and I felt comfortable with him. He reminded me of my math teacher. Like he knew something I didn't and wanted to tell me. Except he was probably two or three years older than me.

"If you say so."

"You like Mexican food?"

"No." I looked away. "I love it." I laughed a little. Why am I so goofy around him?

We found ourselves in Mezcal's and the food was so good. I had tacos and he had quesadillas with a margarita. Every now and again he'd look up at me and my heart would skip. "Russo."

"Huh?" I sipped my virgin pina colada.

"That's my name."

Where have I heard that before? I thought to myself, before scratching my scalp. "Well my name is Amina."

He nodded. "You got a man?"

I thought about Jordan. "No. Not anymore."

"You a cutie."

I pushed back a smile. "Thank you. I guess."

"Why you say it like that?"

I sat back and exhaled. "I guess I don't see myself that way. I had a boyfriend and he started dating my cousin so I must not have been too cute. It's okay though 'cause—"

"He stupid." He interrupted.

"But you don't even know him."

He laughed. "I ain't gotta know him to know he stupid." He winked and picked up his quesadilla before taking a big bite. "I know what I see when I look at you. And if he don't he *dumb*."

I tried to hide my smile but he was making it hard. "If you say so." I shrugged. "I don't see myself like that."

He nodded, wiped his mouth with the back of his hand and sat back in his seat. "I'ma be real with you. On why I wanted to talk. That dude you saw in the alley died."

I almost choked from biting one of the tacos. "Why...why you telling me that?"

"Because he owed some people I know money. And when the cops come, and they will, you ain't see shit. That's all you gotta tell 'em."

"I...uh..."

"You understand what I'm trying to say?"

I nodded yes.

"Good, I don't want you afraid but I want you alive. And to stay alive you have to follow my orders."

Suddenly I had to pee. "I gotta...I gotta go to the—"

"You okay?" He asked.

I nodded yes. "I think so...but can you take me home?"

While sitting in Russo's truck I found out he worked at a car wash not too far from the house. Although he told me everything I wanted to know about him, I kept quiet because I didn't know

By KIM MEDINA

how to feel about seeing somebody before they were killed.

I was scared and almost peed on myself.

When I got out of Russo's ride, Chestnut and her friends were waiting. Russo pulled off and she looked at his truck and walked up to me. I could tell she was mad and finally remembered where I heard his name. She mentioned going to his house when I was in the bathroom and they were outside talking about me.

Please don't let him be her boyfriend.

"What you up to?" She asked, before looking in the direction of Russo's truck.

"'Bout to go in the house and cook for my brother." I paused. "Why?"

"No you not," Chestnut said.

"Why...why you say that?" I cleared my throat.

"Because you coming with us, bitch," Gucci said.

CHAPTER NINE

DRILLO

*D*rillo *looked behind him several times as he walked down the street. When he spotted an alley, he strutted down it positioned a blue milk crate against a brick building, pulled out a gin bottle and drank some.*

It was the same alley of the murder and he even saw the coagulated blood on the ground. Now he understood why the cops had been by earlier asking a bunch of questions. And why Amina kept yelling, "WE AIN'T SEE NOTHING"!

Drillo was going through a hard time in his life and he didn't feel like he could tell anyone. For starters he didn't have any friends, his oldest sister seemed to hate him and his second oldest sister was raped and he couldn't help but feel responsible.

Last night he prayed for some help but stopped midway through because he felt, "stupid". When he remembered his mother kept a secret stash of liquor for her days off, he decided he'd drink it and think of a plan to make things better in his life. And so far the best idea he had was running away like

86   *By KIM MEDINA*

Amina did in D.C., and maybe getting a new family.

He coughed a few times just as Wesley pulled up. He had been following him since he left the house after stealing his mother's secret stash of liquor.

"What you doing, lil nigga?" Wesley asked leaning back in his seat. "'Cause you looking like a creep right now sitting in the alley. Times can't be that hard."

Drillo put the bottle behind his back and stood up. "Who you?"

"You live in that house off Greenmount Avenue?" He paused. "That brick one that's broken down?"

"I gotta go."

Drillo was about to walk past the car when Wesley said, "Don't make me get out."

Drillo sensed that he was a man not to be grappled with so he took a deep breath and said, "I was just drinking that's all."

"I bet your mama don't know about that shit." He paused. "Because I know she would flip the fuck out. All moms do."

Drillo shook his head no. "She at work."

"Well get in anyway. Ride with me somewhere right quick. I live around the neighborhood."

Drillo looked around. "Well I gotta get back to the house first." He pointed up the street. "I told my sister I was going to the store."

"Go back for what? To get told off by her because you drunk? Come on, lil man. It's a nice day. Chill with me. We'll grab some food, maybe some more drinks. The whole nine."

Drillo sighed. "Yeah aight...guess it'll be okay."

When he slid into his dark blue BMW, his spirit told him to leave. To push the door open and run as fast as he could. Although the voice was firm it was also a kind and gentle voice that if he hadn't been still and silent he would not have heard it.

And yet he chose to ignore it.

"You smoke?" Wesley asked, cutting the voice off in Drillo's head instantly.

"Uh...sometimes."

"Which one is it? You smoke or not?"

"No...but I can try."

Wesley lit a blunt that sat in his ashtray already rolled up for the occasion. And said, "Here. Hit it slow. It's that real shit."

"You don't want none?"

By KIM MEDINA

Wesley frowned. "Naw...not right now. That one's all for you. I'm driving."

"That's okay, I'm good." He tried to give it back.

"Smoke up lil nigga. I ain't playing with you. 'Cause right now you acting kind of scared. Like you not your own man or something."

Drillo pouted. "I ain't scared."

"Then do it."

Drillo pulled on the weed and Wesley smiled before placing his hand on Drillo's thigh and pulling off.

CHAPTER TEN

AMINA

My head was killing me. Last night, Chestnut kept pouring liquor down my throat even though I didn't want any more vodka. It was like she was trying to get me sick or maybe even kill me. I started to leave but she kept reminding me that I stood her up the other night so I *owed* her. It wasn't like we were even real friends but she laid the guilt game down thick.

I was lucky my mother was too tired to check on me last night when she got off work because she always knows when I'm doing anything and probably would've smelled the alcohol on my breath.

"Amina and Drillo!" My mother yelled. "Wake up."

I guess she wasn't as tired as I thought last night. I put my pillow over my head and screamed into my bed.

"Amina, did you hear me?" She opened my door. "I made breakfast. Pancakes and corn beef hash. Your favorite. Oh, and I stopped by the mall and picked you up some fresh jeans and new shoes. For school. I had a good tip day last night."

"Thank you."

"But you have to get up. We gotta start early getting this house together."

"Okay ma'am."

"I figured we'd pain the upstairs room and I'm still looking for somebody to do the construction downstairs." She walked in, snatched the pillow off my head. "If we don't fix this house up we violate the agreement and that means we off to Mississippi."

I sat up. "I said I'm up, mama."

She smiled. "I love you, Amina. I see what you doing in Baltimore by trying to make it work here and—"

"AMINA!" Drillo yelled. "JORDAN ON THE PHONE!"

I hopped out of bed and picked it up.

"Five minutes." She pointed at me and walked out.

My heart was pounding and I was so excited I almost forgot to answer. I picked up the house phone and said, "Hello...what...what...how you doing?"

"So you still mad at me?"

I sat on the bed, my body moving under me. "Yes...I mean...I didn't think you were interested in me no more. So I been kinda focusing on my stuff out here I guess."

"So you got a new nigga already?"

"Uh...not really."

"You know what, maybe I shouldn't have called because I know you want to throw in my face that I fucked your cousin. But you know I never loved her like you."

"So you love me?"

"Nah. I mean..."

"Jordan, being with my cousin hurt my feelings but...I...I mean, I figured she was just prettier than me and you liked her more."

"She is prettier, but that's not why I left." He exhaled.

That hurt even more.

"I know she is."

"So now you sound like you wanna cry. You know what, just forget I called." He hung up and my heart dropped. I gave my number to his mother when we first moved in, hoping he would call and he didn't. I know I would never find a better boyfriend and suddenly I didn't feel like doing anything, not even living.

92   *By KIM MEDINA*

We finished painting and I was sitting on the porch watching Drillo in the yard throwing rocks around being an ass. My mother walked up behind me and I could smell her perfume in the air before I saw her. Guess she was leaving for work again.

"Tamika's in the living room watching television," my mother said excitedly. "You should go talk to her. I have a feeling she's coming around and my prayers are working."

"Alright, mama."

"Are you okay?" She paused. "I know Jordan called and—"

"I don't wanna talk about it."

She nodded and then looked at Drillo as if she just remembered something. "Oh yeah, Drillo, you been in my liquor again haven't you?"

He turned around and a guilty look spread on his face. I don't care how he was about to lie because I can tell he did. "What? Nah. I don't want no more liquor. Especially after I got sick that one time."

She activated the alarm. "Maybe I drank more than I thought." She paused. "Look, don't leave this house today." She pointed at both of us. "Spend some time with Tamika and show her you love her. I think she's ready to talk but take it easy on her too."

"We will, ma," Drillo hugged her. "Can I have $5.00?"

"For what?" She slid in her car. "I just told you to stay home. What part about that don't you understand?"

"But I want it for some food."

"Drillo, just stay in the house. There's some chicken wings and fries in there that Amina will cook for you later. And if I find out you been gone when I get back you'll be on punishment."

She pulled off and I stomped in the house. I was still sick from drinking and had tried to call Jordan two more times only for him not to answer. I messed up my big chance with him and now he would probably never reach out again.

I wish I had a cell phone or something. To make stuff more gross I kept thinking about

Russo and if he would hurt me because of the man who got killed.

When I sat back on the sofa I looked over at Tamika. She was sitting up straight and staring at *Real Housewives of Atlanta* on TV. "You watching this stuff?"

"Yes."

My eyes widened because she had been ignoring me since she was raped. I almost forgot what her voice sounded like. "Well I was gonna watch something else," I said. "I'm tired of this show."

She got up and walked away. "Tamika, you can watch it." She kept walking up the stairs. "Tamika, I was just playing dang!" She disappeared into the house. "Fuck!"

"I'ma walk to the store," Drillo said walking back into the house.

"You heard what ma said." I turned the channel. "And if you leave I'ma call her at work."

"Well let me tell this dude out here you can't leave wit' him then." He paused. "Don't make me no never mind."

I jumped up and Russo walked into the house while Drillo smiled and walked out. "Everything cool?" He pointed at my brother.

"Uh...yeah..." I didn't know whether to be scared of him or happy to see him. "He just tripping that's all."

"Well I was stopping by to see if you wanted to go somewhere we could—"

"Let me grab my purse!"

Russo looked over at me while driving down the road. He was giving me the cute smile again but I didn't know if I should embrace it or not. What did he want with me? "Why you come over?"

"I'm taking you shopping."

"You got money to do that?"

He laughed. "Yep."

I looked down at my clothes. "What's wrong with what I have on?"

"I need you to roll somewhere with me."

"So I'm embarrassing to you?"

He laughed. "You wouldn't be in my car if that was the case."

I smiled.

"Do more of that," he said. "You look pretty that way."

I turned my head and covered my mouth. "You laying it on thick."

"I'm telling the truth." He pulled on his strawberry stick again. "So what was you doing before I scooped you?"

"Nothing." I shrugged. "My mother had us painting earlier and then I went downstairs and my sister was acting like a bitch. But that's life as usual on my end so I'm not surprised."

He smiled.

"I'm sorry," I sighed. "I can go off sometimes. You gotta remember not to keep letting me talk so long." I looked at him. "So why you doing all this?"

"Like I said I want you to roll somewhere with me. Plus I felt bad about laying all that on you yesterday." He nodded. "And shit 'bout to be fucked up for you in that house. I want you to remember today when stuff gets rough."

My stomach rumbled.

THE HOUSE THAT CRACK BUILT   97

We came back at night and when I stepped into my house, it was pitch black.

"Drillo!" I yelled into the dark house, bumping over furniture as I moved to the stairs. "Tamika!"

Nobody answered.

In complete darkness I ran upstairs and looked in Tamika's room. She was asleep and seemed annoyed when I crept into her room so I walked back out and searched for Drillo. But he wasn't in his room either. Figuring he was in mama's room, I went there and saw him in the bathroom connected to her room.

Candles lit the space and he was soaking in the tub, blood in the water. His knees were up and he was holding them tightly.

"What happened to you?" I asked covering my mouth. "Why so much blood in there?"

"Nothing happened. I'm fine."

"Drillo! Don't fucking play with me!" I stepped closer and sat on the toilet.

"I got into a fight with my friends." He shrugged. "It ain't nothing to really worry about."

I looked at the bloody water again. "What they do? Cut you or something?"

"No...I just...just punched one of them and they punched me in my lip. Now leave me alone."

By KIM MEDINA

Afraid about everything I was about to walk out when he said, "BGE said mama gotta put the bills in her name before we get electricity again."

I looked at him and nodded. "Oh...okay. You want me to make you something to eat?"

"Nah. Can you close the door please?"

I walked out, not feeling good about what I just saw although I didn't know why. He fought all the time with people on the street, so why would this be different? When I made it to the bottom of the steps I saw a shadow opening and closing cabinets in the living room.

"Who are you?" I yelled at him.

He stopped going through the drawers and stared at me. The whites of his eyes were the only things I could see, the rest of his body was shadowed out. "What you doing here?" He asked, his voice deep with lots of hate. "I ain't never see you in here before. You holding?"

"I'm calling the police!"

He stood up straight and I saw he had a bat in his hand. He moved closer to me. "You better not touch that phone."

I took one step backwards on the stairwell. "Get out!"

He moved closer and now I could see his face inside the darkness. His teeth were chipped and he smelled of dog boo. I was about to take off running when he grabbed my arm and yanked me toward him, the steps digging into my back.

"Hey, Amina you left your—" Russo dropped my purse and walked in the door. "What the..." Russo charged him and grabbed him by the shoulders before punching him in the face. He was about to hit him again when the stranger got up and ran out. "You lock the door. I'ma go chase his ass." He paused. "And why it so dark in here?" He ran out.

I cried on the steps.

By KIM MEDINA

CHAPTER ELEVEN

WESLEY

*T*he sun shined on the green grass as Peter mowed his lawn. The day would've been perfect if his brother Wesley, didn't insist on trailing with clenched fists behind him. Although Peter was doing all he could to ignore him, the sound of the loud engine didn't stop Wesley from spewing words of venom at his sibling.

"And I know you hear me so stop trying to fake like you can't, nigga!" Wesley continued. "I'm not going anywhere until you face me."

"What you want?" Peter yelled.

"Why'd you move somebody in the house you told me you were gonna give me? It ain't right man!"

"On second thought, I can't hear you!" Peter screamed as he continued to push the mower over the grass. "Come back later so we can talk about it then."

Irritated, Wesley moved closer, shoved him to the side and stopped the mower. "Why you sell the house you told me you were going to give me? You ain't 'bout your word at all."

"You already know why." Peter removed his yellow goggles and tossed them to the ground.

"If I did I wouldn't be here."

Peter walked over to the steps of his house and flopped down. Wesley was right on his heels. "Because of mama." He wiped sweat off his brow.

Wesley rolled his eyes. "You don't think she would want me to have the house?" He paused. "I know we had our problems when she was alive but I'm still her son, Pete. And it don't seem right that you carrying stuff this way. Now another family living in there."

"How you figure it's wrong?" Peter paused "She left it in my name." He pointed at himself. "She had three properties and not one was left to you in the will." He pointed at him. "I'm honoring mama that's all."

Wesley looked around. His brother lived in a gated community with enough money to never have to worry about struggling a day in his life. But Stuff was different for Wesley. Much different. Wesley who had always been a dope boy and chosen the darker side of life couldn't say the same. One wrong move and the insignificant life he built for himself would be taken away and he would be hauled off to prison.

102   *By KIM MEDINA*

Still, that didn't stop him from wanting the things he couldn't have. Sure he had fancy cars and a house in the ritzy part of Reisterstown Maryland. But he would never have his mother's love or respect in death or life. That alone had him hating everything, including the world.

"She may have left it in your name but you got a chance to make things right by signing it over. At the end of the day I'm still your brother."

"I'm gonna respect my mother's wishes."

Wesley walked away and walked back. "I will make things difficult for you again." He pointed at him.

"You already tried that. Turned the house that mama built into a dope house a year after she died. Ain't you got no shame?" He paused. "But despite what mama wanted I let you stay in the house after she passed and what did you do? Invite every shameless person within five miles to her home. Well I'm not gonna let you do that again!"

Wesley laughed. "You know what I find hilarious? You and ma acted like she bought that house from working." He paused. "That was the house that crack built!"

"But you put it in her name, Wesley!"

"To hide money! Not to have it taken away. That house belongs to me and I'm not gonna stand by anymore and let you take it. Or act like I did something wrong by giving it to her to hold. Everybody benefited behind me moving crack even you." He pointed at him.

Peter got up and walked into his house as Wesley followed. "I don't know what you talking about."

"Look at your business! You own five apartment buildings and eight houses behind the work I put in on those streets. And now you kicking me to the curb?"

"Two apartment buildings!" Peter pointed in his face. "Remember...the other three you burned down like you did mama's house."

"That wasn't me. I didn't burn mama's house down I keep telling you that." Wesley scratched his head and flopped on the large brown sofa in the room. "And you still own the land those buildings are on."

"Look, I don't want to fight with you."

"Then don't."

Peter put his hand out, palm in Wesley's direction, which was something he hated that he did since they were kids. "You right on some things

By KIM MEDINA

but we men now. To be honest I never asked how you got the money to do the stuff you did for ma and us but let's not forget the bad shit either."

Wesley frowned. "Like what?"

"For starters that other house we grew up in that mama had to put up as bail and lost, because you didn't show up for court. Before you bought the one you want today. Or the bullet wound I got in my back because somebody thought I was you and hit me instead."

"Mama's dead now, Pete. No need in you lying. You knew exactly what I was doing. And you still benefiting."

"What's with that house?" Peter threw his hands in the air. "Why is it so important to you to destroy it?"

Wesley stood up. He walked over to him, placed a hand on his shoulder and sighed. "I spoke more to you about that house than I've done anybody. And you know what? I'm tired of begging." He removed his hand. "You can either hand the house over and let me do what I want, or you know what comes next. We got secrets. Lots of them. You want them coming out?"

Peter swallowed the lump in his throat. "I can't let you have mama's house."

Wesley nodded and walked toward the door. "Then get ready for war."

By KIM MEDINA

CHAPTER TWELVE
TAMIKA

*T*he lights were out and made the room as black as ink as Tamika stared out into openness. It had been months since she endured a savage rape and since she blamed herself, something she hadn't told her family, she elected to keep her voice trapped most times, speaking only when the hurt was too bad on the inside she felt as if she were about to burst.

Although everyone was fast asleep, she was startled when she heard something downstairs. In fear for her life, she pulled the sheets over her head and tried her best to wish the scary thoughts away.

"Get up, Tamika. It's okay." A voice said to her softly in her mind.

The voice was so kind and comforting that she slowly peeled the covers away. The room was empty. "I don't want to, I'm scared."

"There's nothing to be afraid of." The voice continued. "Not anymore."

Tamika sat up and looked around. Everything looked safe but she couldn't be sure. Lately she *heard the voice in the scariest moments but refused to tell her mother for fear that she would put her back on more meds. She knew her mother loved her but the constant asking of questions had Tamika wanting to ignore the world and her problems.*

But something came over Tamika and this time she decided that she wouldn't be afraid. The voice first came to her after days of praying silently for the pain and the memories of the rape to leave her. So she pulled her focus on whatever seemed to be guiding her, while unconsciously separating from her family in the meantime.

Tamika continued down the dark hallway, bare feet pressing into the warped hardwood floors. When she got to the main level, she saw the backdoor was open, causing the glass door to act as a frame to the dilapidated house across from hers. She continued to the door, pushed it open and walked up to a fence that separated hers. She wasn't alone. There was a fifteen-year-old boy that shared her age, seated on a red chair built for a nine year old, eating a sandwich.

His brown skin was soiled with neglect and his clothes weren't fit to be called clothing anymore. But his eyes were kind and despite being taken

By KIM MEDINA

advantage of back home by a male, for some reason she felt comfortable enough to talk to him.

Placing her hands on the cold fence she looked over at him. "You live there?"

He nodded. "Yeah...but I like it more out here." He looked at the sandwich and extended it to her. "Hungry? Want a bite? Got it from Mrs. Connelly across the street." Now she saw his eyes were hazel like honey candy.

She shook her head no. "I ate earlier."

He nodded again, sat the sandwich down and walked over to the gate. They were now eye and eye and both smiled at each other. "I'm glad you did that."

"Did what?" She asked.

"Smile. You look better that way."

She grinned again although she tried not too. "You like living around here?"

"It's bad sometimes, but I'm used to it now I guess." He sighed. "To be honest I didn't think nobody would ever buy this house again. Especially after Jamie went missing before it caught fire."

"Who is Jamie?"

"Let's just say he went through a lot and was abandoned before he showed up missing. Nobody has seen or heard from him since. He was a good friend of mine too. Had deep secrets he didn't wanna tell nobody. Not even me." He paused and looked at the house. "But the house is cursed."

"Why you say that?"

"I used to sit in that chair and watch people do all kinds of stuff. Most of the time they were using drugs but I seen them fight too, have sex out in the open and even kill each other a few times. The police used to be over there all the time before the blaze."

Her eyebrows rose. "When that happen?"

"About a year before you came. Peter ain't tell you before you moved in?"

"I don't think so. I mean, it do smell kind of bad but I just thought it was because it was old." She looked back at it and back at him. "So why you watch people do crazy stuff over here? Ain't you scared? Or got a TV?" She giggled.

"My mother used to have me stand out here and make sure nobody hopped over the fence from your house. It used to happen a lot. But when she started using, I would just watch the house in case I heard her scream and she needed my help. Now...well now she long gone."

By KIM MEDINA

"I'm sorry," Tamika placed her hand over his, which also gripped the fence. "When she die?"

"She not dead like that but it's almost the same." He sighed. "If she gone she still not in my life."

Tamika removed her hand. "Oh. I see."

"She out here somewhere and I just be hoping for that one day when she'll come back, and realize she left me here."

"So who you stay with?"

"Nobody. I'm by myself."

Tamika's eyebrows rose. "Well how you pay the bills?"

"I don't." He laughed. "Guess nobody trying to take this old house away from me. Who else would want to live here? Maybe that's a good thing. You should see the inside. It ain't pretty."

"Well what do you eat?"

"Whatever I can find." He paused. "I got some money saved up though. When I get enough I'm gonna buy a car and go looking for my mother." He dug into his pocket. "Bring her back home because my heart says she needs me wherever she is." He paused. "Hey...what's your name?" He laughed. "I told you everything about me and we don't even know each other's names yet."

She smiled again. "Tamika."

"Well, Tamika I'm Reggie." He paused. "And you know what's funny? I was just asking God that if something was for me, he had to show me because I couldn't see it much anymore. Staying in this house I mean. And then you showed up."

She looked down at herself. "So you think he brought me out here?" She pointed at herself. "I ain't got much to offer nobody."

"It ain't always about what you can offer. Sometimes it's just about talking to a person, and letting them know you listening. You did that more for me tonight than anybody in a long time. And if I can ever do anything for you, I will."

She smiled again. "I wish I had you as a friend months ago."

"What happened?" He frowned.

"I don't talk about it that much. I don't talk at all really." She exhaled. "But...I mean...I gotta go." She turned around and ran.

"Tamika! Wait!"

CHAPTER THIRTEEN

AMINA

He took me to a movie and it was so cute. When I was around Russo I felt like I could do some of the things I wanted to in life, but didn't think I would ever get a chance. Like holding hands. Kissing in public. And even going to school to be a computer programmer. Whenever I told people about my dream they would all laugh because I didn't have a computer and it was what they called the most boring job alive.

We were sitting in his car a few blocks down from my house eating chicken cheese subs so I could see when my mama would pull up and run to the house in time to make her think I never left. She had to work the graveyard shift so I knew I could go out on a date without her knowing. Besides, I really think if she got to know Russo she would like him.

"I gotta ask you something and I want you to be honest," I said smashing my sandwich.

"Can I wait until you stop grossing me out while eating with a mouth full of sub or I gotta hear it now?" He laughed.

"You gotta hear it now."

"'Aight, give it to me." He bit into his food.

"Did I see you jump when that man busted into the bathroom with that knife or was I tripping? I'm just saying."

He almost choked and started laughing. "I didn't think you saw that shit."

"I see everything when it comes to you."

He nodded. "Oh really?"

"Yes, really."

He placed his food down on his lap. "Look, I want to be honest with you about some things."

My appetite left immediately. I knew this wasn't gonna be no fairy tale situation. I'm so stupid. "What is it?" I put my food down in my lap too.

"I'm moving."

"But, I mean, why didn't you say something earlier?"

"To be honest I didn't expect all this."

I positioned my body so I could look at him in the eyes. The sandwich fell to the floor and he tried to pick it up but I stopped him. "Russo, I

By KIM MEDINA

told you about everything bad in my life. About my ex-boyfriend Jordan and you made me feel like..." The words felt useless so I stopped talking.

"I'm sorry."

"I'm so stupid." I unlocked my door and pushed the handle when all of a sudden I was yanked out by my hair and pulled to the cold ground. Somebody was hitting me on the back of the neck and kicking me in my stomach but I couldn't see who it was. I was so tired of everything that after awhile I just gave up fighting and let them have their way.

"Fuck is you doing?" Russo yelled, pulling someone off of me.

When I stood up, my knees burning like fire from scraping on the ground, I saw it was Chestnut and Yolanda. They were huffing and puffing like I did something to them. I was the one who was pulled out of the car, not the other way around.

"What you doing with her?" Chestnut yelled as she stomped up to him. "You belong to me!"

"What did I tell yah ass, huh?" He pointed at her with a stiff finger. "Didn't I tell you to stay away from me? And that it was over? You out here on some creep shit!"

"Russo, please don't do this," she said softly. "You know I would never step to you if you didn't have another girl in the truck."

"But we not together!" He yelled. "What part are you not getting? I can have whoever in my truck I fucking want!"

She frowned and clenched her fists again, while staring in my face like I did something. "So now you think you gonna be with her? The new girl in the neighborhood? While my friends and everybody know you playing me?"

"Whatever I decide to do is my business."

"You wrong as fuck," Yolanda said.

"Yo, shut the fuck up, bird!" He yelled at her. When he was done he walked over to me. "You okay?"

I nodded before looking at Chestnut, Yolanda and Gucci who were all staring at me. "Yeah, I think so."

He moved closer and put his hands on my shoulders. "Walk home and I'ma stop by later to check on you."

I nodded. "You gonna be fine?" I asked, although I didn't know why.

"And if he not?" Chestnut said putting her hands on her hips. "What you gonna do about it 'cept get your ass stomped?"

Russo shoved Chestnut back again. "Just go home, Amina. I got all this over here."

I nodded and ran away.

On my way home all I could think about was how stupid I was to believe somebody like Russo could want me in the long term. We didn't have sex and he didn't ask for it either but still my mind and heart hurt just thinking that I could like a person so much, only for them to be leaving before we could have a chance.

AGAIN!

Before it happened I was starting to think maybe I wasn't ugly and...you know what...I'm tired of this shit. I'm tired of feeling sorry for myself and I'm tired of people not wanting me for whatever reason. If Russo gotta leave than so be it. It's time to start thinking of myself.

Fuck these niggas out here in these streets.

When I got home I saw Tamika in the living room looking at the television even though it was off. I didn't have time for her either and I was about to walk up stairs when she said, "He said he needed help with his chair. And that he wanted me to grab the other end so it could be easy putting it in the van."

I closed the door and slowly walked over to where she sat.

"I didn't believe him and a voice told me not to go but he looked so sad." Tears rolled down her cheeks. "Like he...like he couldn't hurt me even if he tried."

I moved closer, but was careful not to interrupt her with stupid responses. This was the first time she told anybody about what happened which that night was why nobody could find the person who raped her. She didn't even give us a description of how he looked.

"So I took the back of the chair and he took the front and then he pushed me inside," she cried harder, her voice booming through the house.

"Like in a movie I saw one time," I said in a whisper.

"When I was in the van he punched me in the face and...and...made me lick his thing and do a lot of other stuff. I begged him to stop but he said if I didn't he would kill mama, you and Drillo. And I...I just..." She broke down harder and I held her in my arms.

The Night She Was Raped

"Girl, I don't care if you like him or not he gross," Tamika said to her friend who she was walking down the street with, on the way to the store.

"Gross as in ugly or...?" Vanisha asked.

Tamika laughed. "Gross...ugly...all of it."

Vanisha rolled her eyes. "You may think he's gross but—"

"VANISHA, WHERE THE FUCK DO YOU THINK YOU GOING?" Vanisha's mother yelled. The girls turned around to see her wearing a white silk nightgown that was being teased by the warm wind that came through.

"I was just going to the store with Tamika."

"Bitch, you better get your ass in this house." She pointed at her with a lit cigarette between her fingers. "And if Tamika got any sense she'll go in the house too. This neighborhood ain't fit for two girls walking alone at night."

Vanisha turned around to Tamika. "Sorry, 'Mika."

"NOW"! Her mother yelled.

Vanisha took off running to her house. After realizing the hike was too far to go alone, she turned back around. She was in front of her house when a small black man holding his arm walked up to her right before she went into the building.

"Hey, young lady," He paused. "You mind helping me put this couch in the van?"

Don't go. The voice said in her head. *It's not safe.*

"Uh...I..."

"It'll be real quick, young lady. I hurt my arm and can't do much for myself." He rubbed it for effect. "Please."

Tamika looked at her building and from where she was, she could hear her mother going off through the open window about something on the phone.

"Please." He persisted, feeling as if he may lose her.

Tamika smiled and said, "Okay. I guess it'll be fine."

"Great," he clapped his hands once and looked around. "You take the back end of the recliner and I'll take the front."

Just as he said, Tamika positioned herself behind the recliner as he took the front. Slowly she backed up until she was hidden by the inside of the van with nowhere to go. When she tried to get around it, he punched her in the face so quickly she didn't know what happened. Flat on her back, she released a small yell before he slammed his callous hand over her mouth and moved his face close to hers. Little did they both know that Amina was on the outside of the van and heard the noise, although she didn't know what she was tuning in too.

Once he was on top of her he removed his penis, tore off her panties since she was wearing a dress, and raped her. With a hand still over her mouth he said, "If you say anything I will kill everybody in your family."

Satisfied she would remain silent he removed his hand, raped her in the anus, the vagina and mouth. She was in excruciating pain and couldn't believe she allowed herself to be lured by a stranger. Her mother warned her about men like him and there she was, on her back, being assaulted.

When he was done he smiled at her. "Stupid, little bitch. You wanted me to do this didn't you? That's why you were walking alone."

Tamika remained silent. Angry at her attitude, he stole her in the face.

Thinking she was unconscious he bolted out the van's door. A little lightheaded, she scooted halfway out but the pain in her head was too much to handle. Right before her feet hit the ground she passed out, her feet dangling out of the vehicle.

"I'm so sorry, Tamika." Her cries were heavy and for some reason I cried too. It was so loud I thought we would wake mama up until I remembered she wasn't home. "I'm sorry I wasn't there for you and I'm sorry he made you do those things. But I...I love you. Mama does too. And you gonna be okay."

By KIM MEDINA

She squeezed me harder. "Now I'm afraid. I'm afraid to live and I'm afraid to die. What am I gonna do?"

"I don't know." She separated from me and looked into my eyes. "Maybe we gotta take one day at a time." I shrugged. "Maybe we gotta just, see what happens next and...and...live."

"I don't think I can..."

I took a deep breath. "Maybe you don't have to make no decisions right now, 'Mika. Maybe all you gotta do is ..." I jumped up when I saw someone staring in the back door. His figure looked black and I was horrified. "What the—"

"Are you okay, Tamika?" The person asked. When I blinked a few times I saw him clearer. He was tall but dirty and I wondered who he was. "I heard you screaming."

She stood up and walked toward the door. "Yeah...I'm fine though. Just talking to my sister."

He nodded. "Good, I heard you crying and wanted to make sure." He smiled. "Well, good night."

"Good night."

He walked off.

"Who was that?" I asked still shaking.

"So you saw him too?" She asked.

"Yeah."

"Before you saw him I thought he was an angel." She smiled. "But he's even better than that." She walked upstairs with a smile on her face.

CHAPTER FOURTEEN

PAM

P *am followed Peter around the house as he examined every nook and cranny. As she watched him move she noticed his face had been badly beaten and wondered who he'd gotten wrong to deserve such a whipping.*

When he was done he stood in the living room looking disappointed. "Okay, it's been weeks and this is not what we discussed. You have made no progress whatsoever!"

"I know but I—"

"This is a business." He threw his hands up. "And you aren't following our agreement in the least."

"I know but you have to understand. I got three kids and I work one and a half full time jobs." She paused. "I'm doing the best I can with the time I've been given."

"I'm sorry, but am I your lover?" He pointed at himself.

"What?" She frowned. "No!"

"So why are you burdening me with all this?"

Pam flopped on the seat. "I know what you're saying is true but I was hoping you'd find some compassion."

"Wasn't it compassion that gave you the rate I did on this house? Don't be so ungrateful!"

She nodded her head. "I guess you're right, Peter. It just seems like you're dead set on getting us to do work that should only impact us right?"

"Meaning?"

"Am I confused or did you promise to let us rent to own the property once the repairs were done?" He paused. "And didn't you say that you were only making us do that so that we would pass inspection come settlement time? So who cares what progress we make?"

"We are not in a relationship, Pam. We are in a business situation and I need this house to be repaired or you'll have to pay full rent." He pointed down at the floor. "My reasons have nothing to do with anything else."

"And how much is that? The rent if we don't make the repairs."

He exhaled. "One thousand a month."

She jumped up. "One thousand dollars a month! Are you crazy? Do you know how many *rats and roaches we killed this morning alone? This place is a dump!"*

"You wanted to be here remember?"

"Okay, Peter, whatever you say. Just give me some time to work this all out." He was about to leave when she asked, "What happened to your face? Is someone trying to get you to sell the house to them?"

"Just finish what you agreed to do and let me worry about everything else." He walked out the door.

AMINA

I was in a better mood even though I hadn't heard from Russo and I didn't see Chestnut and her friends at school. I couldn't be sure but maybe it was talking to Tamika yesterday.

All that changed the moment I walked into the house. My mama was standing in the living room pacing and a police officer was sitting on the sofa glaring at me. He stood up when he saw me and my heart dropped.

"Where's Drillo?" I asked, worried he got into some trouble.

"He's over a friend's house." Mama said softly. "But that ain't what this is about."

I exhaled. "So what's wrong?"

"I think you know what's wrong, Amina." Mama said before walking over to me. "Now do you want to explain or continue to play these games?"

"I'm...I'm..." Words wouldn't leave my mouth as I struggled to find the right thing to say. "I'm confused."

"This officer is here because someone reported seeing a girl walk into Mrs. Connelly's house down the street. And they stole a cell phone out of her house."

I shrugged. "Okay? I helped her one time to take her groceries in but I haven't been back since. What all this got to do with me?"

"So how can you explain this phone?" The officer raised it in the air. "Your mother found it in your room, after I placed a call to it and it rang from under your pillow."

I stumbled backwards. "Wait...I didn't do anything like that! I would never take something from somebody else. Especially not an old lady."

By KIM MEDINA

"Amina, you been asking me for a phone for months. What you expect me to do?"

"I expect you to believe me."

She looked at me long before folding her arms over her chest. "I'm afraid we're way past that now." She sighed. "Luckily this nice officer has talked Mrs. Connelly into not pressing charges. But you grounded for two weeks."

"For what?" I yelled. "This is so wrong! You believing somebody without even hearing me out."

"I just gave you a chance to explain yourself!"

"Ma, I didn't do this."

"Well I'm about to leave," the officer said to my mother. "I'll take Mrs. Connelly's property to her." He looked at me. "You're lucky to have such a nice neighbor. She's one of the few people who still believe in this town. I happen to believe it's a death trap myself, void of hope and love." He walked out.

I walked up to my mother. "Mama, I didn't do this."

"Amina, just go to your room. With everything I have going on I can't do any of this with you right now."

"Mama, I didn't—"

"Are you crazy? Or do you think everybody that dumb? The phone was in your room, Amina! How on earth can you explain that?" She paused. "Do you realize Peter is trying to throw us out if we don't fix up this house? He's afraid it'll be condemned and you and your brother haven't even tried to paint the areas I assigned to you weeks ago. Instead both of you stay out in the street leaving all of this on me." She tossed her hands up in the air. "Do you want to leave for Mississippi?"

"No, but what I'm tired of doing is running. Your answer for everything is to pick up and leave and that's not fair to us."

"So what's the plan? Stay with my sister who too busy whoring herself to care about us?"

"No! But—"

"Amina, just go upstairs." She flopped on the sofa and placed her face in her hands. "I'm not about to have this conversation with you. Plus, my migraines are coming on again."

"Mama, I—"

"JUST GO!"

I looked at her once again and ran upstairs. My mind was twirling about who could have set me up but I was coming up short. When I got to my room I heard someone calling my name in the backyard and when I looked out the window it was Chestnut and Yolanda.

I immediately got my answer.

"How you like your new phone?" Chestnut said. "I noticed you didn't have one so we arranged for you to get it."

I opened the window. "Why you do that?" I whispered heavily. "I could've gotten locked up."

She pulled a knife from her pocket. "Worry about this slice I'ma give you on the face the next time I catch you outside. You ain't 'bout to get with him so get that out yah head."

My heart dropped. "Why you doing all this?"

"Russo's off limits." She said. "And now you know." They both ran away, laughing the whole time.

CHAPTER FIFTEEN

AMINA

Mama asked me to go grocery shopping earlier because her head hurt. I didn't want to because I wasn't sure if Chestnut would make good on slicing my face but I didn't have a choice. If she knew I was scared to live around the neighborhood she would definitely make us leave and that's the last thing I needed right now.

When I made it to my house, I saw Drillo coming out with Wesley, the guy Chestnut and them said to stay away from. Drillo was tucking something in his pocket and Wesley was smiling from ear to ear. I also noticed that Drillo was wearing new shoes. Where he get them from? Was he slinging dope?

I rushed up to the steps. "What you doing in my fucking house?" I asked Wesley.

"You a small girl to have such a big mouth." He said. "Maybe you should work on that. It makes you unattractive."

"He was just giving me some—"

"Drillo, go in the house!" I yelled.

"But I was—"

"Take these bags in the house and go!" When he snatched them out my hands and walked away I focused on him. "Who are you and what do you want? I mean, I saw you creeping past here not too long ago and now you coming out the house with my little brother. If it's money you after you coming to the wrong place. We broke around these parts."

"Do I look like I need paper?" He raised his hands and my eyes focused on the chain dangling on his neck. The sun shining it up real good. "I'm here because I can make your problems go away. You should be kissing the tops of my sneaks."

"That's funny, you don't know me so that means you can't know my problems."

"Let me guess."

I crossed my arms over my chest. "I'm listening."

"You gotta repair this dump or move. Plus you got some problems with the nigga Russo on account of him fucking with the girl Chestnut before you moved on the block. She trying to ruin that cute little red face of yours. Am I right yet?"

I dropped my hands down by my sides. "How you know all that?"

"Does it matter?" He asked. "It's true right?"

"I was told not to trust you." I frowned. "And I think they right."

"But look who told you that. The person who framed you with a phone you didn't take." He paused. "Now you tell me, who's the real enemy?"

"What were you doing in my house?" I frowned. "I'm still not getting the answer to my question."

"Well like I said, I hear you need repairs and I'm willing to help. I own a construction company but I'll do the work mostly myself if your people want." He paused. "Your brother kind of likes it around here and he wanted to know if I could do anything. Now normally I don't get involved in personal matters but I had a change of heart."

Something didn't sound right. "What you want out of it?"

"Nothing, just mentoring the kid that's all. Baltimore can be tough. You need friends around here." He shrugged. "Look, I know they told you not to trust me, but if you got to know me you'd see I'm a good guy."

Mama said whenever somebody says they are a good person not to believe them. I think she right but we in a bind.

"I don't know about all that."

By KIM MEDINA

He laughed. "I'm your best hope, girly. Besides, the way things are panning out for you right now what do you really have to lose?"

TAMIKA

Tamika and Reggie were sitting in broken down lawn chairs in her yard. He reached into the stash he saved to buy them a small pizza with sodas and they were sharing it under the sun, a cool breeze relaxing them even more.

"This is so good," Tamika said rubbing her belly. "How'd you know I'd like it?"

"Pizza's a no hater food." He opened his soda.

"What that mean?"

"Think about it, how many people you know can turn down a slice of pizza? It hardly happens. Ever."

She thought about it and said, "You know what, I think you right."

She looked at the sky, above the broken down homes that surrounded them. "So when you gonna go? To look for your mother?"

He shrugged. "I don't know. I got nine hundred seventy five dollars saved up but I can't afford a car with that. I need to collect a little more."

Her eyes widened. "So you got all that money and you not spending none of it on..." She looked him over. His clothes and shoes were filthy but his face and hands were clean.

He laughed.

"I'm sorry, Reggie." She said softly. "I didn't mean to be...mean. I don't care what you wearing to be honest."

He nodded. "I know. I can tell that about you." He paused and looked down at himself. "I figured clothes get old and ain't worth much after a while anyway. But family's forever. That's why I haven't spent none on myself." He looked into her eyes. "Can I tell you something?"

"Yeah." She moved uneasily in her seat. "Go ahead."

"I watch your mother sometimes through the kitchen windows. The way she does stuff for you like smooth out your hair to make sure it's nice. Or scrape your toast off since you don't like it black. Or sings and cooks your meals."

Her eyes widened and she giggled. "Wow. This should really be creeping me out right now."

"I'm serious. You lucky. A lot of people out here ain't got—"

"You know what, I'm done talking about my mother." She shook her head. *"Since your mother...you know."*

Tamika put her hand over her heart. *"But it doesn't bother me. Really. I like to hear you speak."*

He nodded. *"But I want to hear you talk. You wanna tell me why you ran away from me the other day?"* He paused. *"Open up to me, Tamika. Why you got all that sadness in your eyes?"*

"I can't right now." She looked away. *"And I know I can with you eventually but I can't right now. That's gotta be enough."*

He smiled. *"Gotchu, gotchu."*

"Why you smiling though?" She asked.

"Because I think you gonna be mine."

"Be your what?" She giggled.

"Miss Tamika, we too young to be playing games. You know exactly what I mean."

She laughed louder. *"How come you act old?"*

He looked around and sighed. *"Baltimore can do that to a man I guess. It's the only place in the world where you can be right in the middle of the worsts times of your life, and then find the best* moments. *Either way you have to be ready for both.*" He looked at her. "*I feel that when I'm with you.*" He shrugged. "*I know I talk old but...if you seen the stuff I have you'd get it. You'd get me.*" He paused. "*At the end of the day I'm just trying to heal.*"

"*Maybe we can do that together.*" She touched his hand. "*What you think?*"

"*I want that for us. Bad.*"

CHAPTER SIXTEEN

AMINA

Drillo and me were taking painting supplies from the cab we caught from Home Depot and into the house. When Tamika walked around from the back, I smiled until I saw the guy who came to the door standing next to her. Even though he was wearing a holey black t-shirt and very soiled jeans, his eyes were nice and it made me change my approach from when he stepped to the door.

Kinda.

I paid the cab, walked up to them and said, "Who's this, Tamika?"

"He's my friend." She looked at him and smiled and I was almost knocked back. I couldn't remember the last time I saw her this happy.

If ever.

"Reggie," he said extending his hand. "Can I help you with anything?"

"No, I'm good." I shook it.

"Sorry about that night when I looked through the door," he paused. "I just wanted to make sure Tamika was okay." He looked at her.

"Wow...so this seems awfully....cute."

Tamika giggled and then looked behind me. "Who's that?"

When I turned around I saw Russo pulling up. He got out of the truck and walked over to me. He looked and smelled so good with his designer jeans and fresh white t-shirt that I wondered how he made that kind of money at the car wash. Even his long braids were recently done. "Look, I know I haven't been by since—"

"I don't have nothing to say to you."

"Wow...really?"

"I'm tired of people treating me like a non factor." I sighed. "So if you want to mess with that girl and you moving to New York, just do it. I got stuff here to worry about anyway. Don't need no more trouble."

"Let me take you out." He walked closer and grabbed my hand. "And if I don't win you over you don't ever have to talk to me again. You can't beat that."

"Nah...I'm good." I snatched my hand away.

"Amina, I know it was wrong but I'm not dealing with that girl. You heard how I went at her, in front of you." He paused. "If I knew she was about to do what she did I would've never

140 *By KIM MEDINA*

had you out there like that. We had a moment back in the day, it was over and now she don't know how to deal with it." He paused. "Let me take you out." I rolled my eyes. "Is there anything I can do to get you to change your mind?"

I looked behind me at Tamika and Reggie who were also waiting for an answer. "Okay, I'll go, but you got to take them with us."

Tamika and Reggie grinned hard.

An hour later the four of us were on our way to this surprise place that Russo didn't want to tell us about. Before leaving, we stopped by the mall to get Reggie and Tamika some new clothes to wear for the day and he even got Reggie a fresh haircut. Every time I glanced in the back seat at my sister I saw them holding hands and whispering. Reggie was definitely a snack now that he was fresh and I could see why my sister liked him.

When we pulled up to the place for our date it was a sky diving building and I almost shit my drawers.

"Oh my God!" Tamika yelled. "I always wanted to do this."

Reggie shrugged. "I never thought about it but I'll try anything once." They both left the car and I looked over at Russo.

"I don't know about this," I said, my heart beating out of my chest. "This not exactly my idea of a good time. I think I'm about to pass out in here."

He touched my hand. "I know."

"So why bring me here?"

He sighed. "I know all you can think about is me going to New York. But I think if it's meant to be together than we gonna be. And I want you to always have memories with me that no body can change or stand next to. I want to be original with you...always."

I looked out the window at Tamika and Reggie kissing.

"Dude, is official," he said. "I remember when he wasn't on hard times. He used to look after his mother and his house and make sure she was good, even when the drugs took her over. Your

By KIM MEDINA

sister chose right with dude. I forgot he was even still around here because he not in the streets."

I looked at Russo. "Why do you always take people shopping and stuff before going out?"

"Man, I remember when I didn't have money to buy clothes and stuff." He paused. "No matter what I was doing, even if it was something that should've been fun, I was too busy caring about how I looked. By changing the clothes on a person, for a moment anyway, you can put how bad you really feel away for a minute and just have fun."

My heart skipped. I wanted him so badly now I couldn't stand to see him go to New York or anywhere for that matter. "I wish you wouldn't leave."

"I know...but I don't want you getting mad at me either. So for now let's just enjoy each other. Okay?"

When we got out I walked slowly to the door to the building. Everybody else was happy, laughing and smiling but I felt like I could throw up if I stood long enough in the corner. I was just about to walk out and wait in the car while they got suited up with their body harnesses when Russo grabbed my hand softly.

THE HOUSE THAT CRACK BUILT   143

"Trust me."

In that moment I thought about what did I really have to lose? So I got suited up and waited while we boarded a small plane, stomach still twirling. Even flying to the right altitude to leap was racking my nerves so I just focused on my sister who was sitting happily with Reggie and Russo, who looked at me as if I were the only person on the planet.

Suddenly I didn't care.

And then my instructor who I was connected to asked, "are you ready to jump?"

I nodded even though I wasn't and before I knew it we leaped into the air. At first I was screaming and yelling but then calmness came over me. I told myself even if I dropped to my death when it was all said and done, wouldn't it be sad if I didn't look around at the clouds and the ice blue sky? My ears popped a little at first but then I felt light and free and I started crying. It was the best time of my life and I never felt so free and seen anything so beautiful. When I looked to my right I saw Russo with his instructor and also my sister and Reggie with theirs.

I couldn't help but wonder if by the four of us doing something so amazing that maybe we

144   *By KIM MEDINA*

would be tied in life together. And the way I was feeling right now, I would not have a problem with that.

I was...well...happy.

Mama was right. Maybe Baltimore would change my life for the better.

CHAPTER SEVENTEEN

AMINA

Lately me, Russo, Tamika and Reggie had been inseparable. Drillo would hang out with us every so often, when he knew we were going to dinner, but for the most part he was hanging with his friends in the neighborhood even though nobody ever saw them.

But now it was back to reality.

Today was the day that we decided to start most of the work for the basement. Mama was still trying to find somebody to do the repairs since we didn't tell her, mostly because we wanted it to be a surprise.

Today Wesley used me, Tamika, Reggie and Drillo to do some of the work while he directed us and brought in a nice Mexican man name Carlos for the harder jobs.

We were almost getting stuff done when mama came home early, something she had been doing a lot of lately. Before going back to work recently she stayed off to try and do all she could but the basement was just too tough to do alone. She

By KIM MEDINA

figured she would go back to work until she could come up with another plan.

But we solved that problem for her by bringing in Wesley.

"What's going on?" She asked walking down into the basement.

Wesley placed a piece of wood against the wall, dusted off his hands on his pants and walked up to her. "I'm Wesley."

Mama looked at his hand and didn't shake it. "And who are you?"

"I'm a friend of your kids. And they are doing something very nice for you."

Mama looked at us. "What are you doing here?"

"Well I was told you needed help with your project. And since I'm a friend of the neighborhood I decided to pitch in."

Mama placed her hands on her hips. "I don't trust you. Something tells me you mean my family no good. It's all in your eyes."

"No good?" Wesley smiled. "Ma'am, you're in a bind and all I want to do is lend a hand. But if you're opposed to help I can always leave. It's not a problem. Just say the word."

Mama looked at us. "He's really good, ma." Drillo said. "And we getting stuff done now. So Pete can stay off your case. Might as well let him stay. Look at how much we finished."

Mama looked at me and I looked away. I learned from my new relationship with Russo alone that when Mama felt something, nine times out of ten she was right. Plus I didn't like Wesley much either.

"You know what, it looks like you have things under control so I'll leave." Wesley headed for the stairs.

"Wait..." Mama said. "Come back, young man."

Wesley turned around. "Yes."

"If you sure you want to help, I could use it."

Wesley walked up to her and extended his hand. This time she shook it. Because she had too. "We have a deal."

"I don't make much but maybe I can pay you something when I'm having a better day at the restaurant." Mama said.

"Don't worry about that. Just make me a few meals and that'll work."

"Okay, if you say so."

"I just remembered something is in my car I have to grab it." Wesley said. "I'll be right back."

When he left we all walked up to mama. "I'm staying here for the next couple of days," she said. "Something tells me he means no good but God uses even the wicked for a day of good." She paused. "Don't see why this should be much different."

There was a knock at the back door. When I answered it was Russo looking and smelling so good. I let him in and he walked up to mama. "This is Russo, mama. The guy I was telling you about."

She smiled. "Nice to meet you, son. I've heard a lot of nice things about you. From everybody." She looked at Tamika's boyfriend. "Even Reggie can't stop singing your praises. I hope it's all true."

"Thank you, ma'am." He smiled.

"Well let me put my things down so I can get started on this house." She walked up the stairs.

Russo dapped up Reggie, hugged my sister and then softly pulled me away. "Can I talk to you in private?"

"Why you ain't tell me Wesley was coming by here?" He asked me outside in the backyard. "I would have vetoed that situation like yesterday."

"Vetoed the situation? What's wrong?"

"Bae, that dude is the worst. You gotta stay away from him."

"Well right now we gotta fix the house so we can stay here. And he said he knows how. Already we got more done with him than we did without him."

"You want some money?" He asked. "Because I can maybe grab some from my people at work to get stuff done for you around here. I don't want you depending on him for shit."

"No. I mean, I want to do this the right way."

"And you think that's the right way by fucking with that dude?" He pointed at Wesley's truck. From where we were we could see him loading stuff in a toolbox. "That dude is a—"

"Russo, this is not the argument for you to fight me on." I said firmly, placing my long hair behind my ear. "Really."

"What's that 'sposed to mean?"

"It's like you avoid all other conversations with me. Stuff having to do with me and you being together. But now you wan to talk my head off about Wesley and fixing the house?"

"Bae, I'm just trying to tell you he's a—"

"Just leave it alone, Russo! Please!"

He nodded, sighed and grabbed my hands. "You right...I don't want this for us." He paused. "The four of us still on for the movies tonight right?"

"Yeah, that's all Reggie keep talking about."

"Oh yeah, let me go rap to him 'bout something real quick." He kissed me. "I gotta make a few runs after that so I can't stay long."

When he walked in the house Wesley walked up to me. "So you two an item now huh? You with the big man on the streets."

"What you trying to say?"

He moved closer. "I don't know what's there not to get. You a hustler's wife."

I laughed. "Russo don't deal drugs."

"Wait...you being serious?" He said. "That man actually got you thinking he on the straight and narrow?"

"He gotta job."

"Listen, ask anybody on the block who moving more dope than enough first. Bet your man's name come up." He moved even closer. "And in case you wondering, the nigga that got killed in the alley when ya'll first moved around here, when the cops were asking questions, well that murder was on his word. Stay woke and you'll know what I'm saying is true."

Later that day I stopped by Mrs. Connelly's house. She was standing in the yard when she saw me walk up. "Please don't be afraid. I just want to ask you something.

"I'm not afraid of you."

"Even after the people said I stole your phone?"

"I'm not dumb, Amina." She paused. "I know that wasn't in your nature."

I smiled.

"Why you think I told the people not to press charges?" She continued.

"Mrs. Connelly, you been around here for a long time. Is Russo a drug dealer?"

She laughed. "The biggest one I've ever seen. But the real monster is that Wesley character you've been keeping time with. I don't know why you guys let him in your home, but I can tell you this. You'll come to regret it dearly."

CHAPTER EIGHTEEN

AMINA

I stomped down the block toward Russo's house mad at the world and everybody in it. I was so angry that I forgot about the threat that Chestnut made to cut me in the face if she caught me walking alone, something that never left my mind for a long time.

When I made it to his house he was outside washing his truck. He smiled when he saw me, placed the rag on the car and moved up to me. "Hey, beautiful. This a treat."

"Are you a drug dealer?" I yelled.

He looked around and pulled me closer. "What you talking about? You high or something?"

"Russo, do you deal in drugs?" I slapped the back of my hand into my palm.

"What...huh...why...if...come on...what you talking about?"

I frowned. "What are you even saying right now? I asked you a question and you clearly beating around the bush. I guess I got my answer though."

"How come whenever we 'bout to hang out and do something fun, you gotta ruin it with all the questions and conversations? Females be killing me with that shit. Just roll with it."

"I need an answer and I need it right now."

"Amina."

"Russo!" I yelled. "Just be honest! For once. I don't want to hear it from someone else. Now if we friends, and if you care about me even a little bit just tell the truth."

He looked down. "Ride with me somewhere."

"Will I get my answer?"

"You sure will."

I got in his truck and twenty minutes later, it was like the houses went from leaning on one another in my neighborhood, to being so far apart you could scream and nobody would hear you. When we finally pulled up to a house, he put in a code and the gates opened, allowing us inside.

"Russo, what's this?" My eyes were so wide they hurt.

"Just chill, bae. I promise to tell you everything you want to know." He put his hand on my leg. "Trust me. There's nothing to be afraid of."

He parked his truck behind two BMW's. One was white and the other was black with tinted windows. We got out and he held my hand and led me to two large wooden doors. When they opened we stepped inside and everything was brown and gold.

It was epic.

"Russo, whose house is this?" It was like I was standing in the middle of a celebrity's mansion.

"Oh, Mr. Lewis, you're home," A Spanish woman with a wide smile greeted him. "Can I get you anything?"

"Yes, bring me and my friend two cokes. We'll be in the living room."

He led me to a room so glamorous I felt nervous sitting anywhere for fear I would knock something over. "Russo, this is scaring me." We sat on a plush cream sofa.

He took a deep breath and said, "Now, to answer your question. Yes, I deal a little."

I coughed. "A little?"

"You know what I mean."

"Nah, I don't. Why bring me here to cut corners? You could've just left me on the block."

"I deal in coke. Lots of it."

I nodded. "So it's true that the man who was in the alley—"

"He tried to rob me and I had to handle him."

I backed away. "So you...so you had somebody killed?"

He moved closer. "Amina, I don't make the murder moves my first moves. But when someone tries to disrespect you have to retaliate. That's the level of the business I'm in. There's no way around it."

"But I...I...thought you had a job at that car wash. I saw you there cleaning cars and everything."

"I own that spot and pitch in every now and again to save face."

"But...what about the house in my neighborhood?"

"I stay there to make sure shit moves smooth but I sleep here. Always."

I got up. I heard enough. "Take me home."

He followed. "Amina, please hear me out. I never brought anybody here. Not Chestnut, not another female, not anybody. EVER! I don't even know why I'm doing it now except I...I think I'm..."

My eyes widened. "What, Russo?" Tears rolled down my face.

"No...I know I love you. Ain't no thinking in it."

It was the first time anybody had ever said it and my body trembled. "You do?"

"Yes, it's like I watched you grow in such a short period of time and it's like...I want to support that. I want to take care of you and show you a life that you can't even imagine in your biggest dreams. I know you can't see things my way right now but, but, I just want you to try. Please." He walked up to me and kissed me. "Please..." He kissed me again and snaked his arms around my back. "Please, baby. Don't leave me. Just give it a chance."

Some kind of way we ended up in his room. The bed was so large it could hold six twin beds side by side. He slowly removed my jeans, and then my shirt leaving me in my underwear. "Russo, I'm scared." Next he removed my bra and panties and stared down at my body.

"You're perfect." He said as he lay on top of me.

My legs widened and suddenly he was inside of me. It felt so good and so right. He was so hard, so warm and so passionate and I realized I

By KIM MEDINA

never made love before in my life. He kissed my neck, the sides of my face and then my lips as he continued to move in and out of my wet pussy.

I didn't know what was in store for us but I knew he would be in my life, in one way or another forever. "I love you too." I whispered. "So much."

He smiled. "Good, 'cause at first I thought you were never gonna say it." He pumped a little harder. "But I'm glad you did."

We made love for two hours and when we were done he walked me outside and handed me a set of keys. "Take the white one out front."

My eyes widened. "Wait...the BMW?"

"You can drive right?"

"Yeah...but...I...what if I mess it up?"

"Then fuck it, I'll buy another one." He paused. "If you dealing with me this is your new life. Get used to it and stunt on them bitches hard."

AMINA

Amina cruised down the street in Russo's BMW like she owned the world. She could definitely get used to this life. When she came to a light she glanced at herself in the mirror. She went to the Dominicans and had her hair pressed which caused her true mane to run even longer down her back. She even let the stylist throw a little makeup on, to present the new Amina and how she was feeling.

She was a long way from the girl who left DC and she loved it too. Her eyes were different. The way she held her head up was different and the way she was dressed. Russo had also given her a few bucks and she decided to stop by a few neighborhood stores to shine, in case she ran into people she knew.

She got her wish.

She was too excited when she went to the mall and saw Jordan and her cousin fighting in the food court as she herself, held a rack of shopping bags.

"Amina," Jordan said. "Is that you?"

She smiled. "Oh, hello J and April. I'm glad to see ya'll still making it."

He looked at April and rolled his eyes. "So...who you with now?"

"You don't know him. He from Baltimore. His name's Russo."

Jordan looked like he was about to shit himself. "Russo the plug?"

That was the first time Amina realized who she was dealing with. Russo had done such a good job of making himself look like everybody else, that she still didn't get the gist of whom she was dealing with until that moment. Her dude was put on in the best ways.

"Yeah...that's him." She winked. "But let me get out of here. Yah keep doing what yah do." She switched out of the mall.

Little did she know someone else was watching her and was heated at it all.

Chestnut.

CHAPTER NINETEEN

AMINA

For the past few weeks so much good had been happening in my life. Russo and me were spending more time together, and every time he picked me up he looked at me like he loved me so much he was about to explode. Reggie and Tamika were doing good too and Reggie had started spending time with Russo alone.

Stuff was going too smooth in my world and I tried to tell myself not to expect the worst. Mama said whenever a man expects the worst instead of the best; God has to show him what he asked for so he'll know for future reference.

I sure hope that's not true.

I just walked into the house after being with Russo all day at his luxury home. Some man came to the door and Russo told me to grab my clothes we bought from Saks Fifth Ave and he'd see me at home. When I opened the door, I saw my mother sitting in the living room alone. She cut the TV off.

"Amina, come sit next to me."

I sat the bags on the sofa while trying to determine if I should fake a stomachache to get out of it or not. "Is everything okay?"

"Drillo, Tamika and Reggie went to McDonalds." She paused. "They caught a cab. But I told them if they waited you could take them but they acted like they didn't know what I was talking about."

"Me either...I..."

"I know about the car, Amina. Mrs. Connelly saw you driving in it yesterday and the day before that. Said you were parking it in front of her house to avoid me knowing. Is this the kind of life you want?"

"What kind of life?" I cleared my throat.

"The dope life, baby. A life of never feeling like you deserve a thing because it didn't come by you the right way. The honest way. You using people's soul money."

I sighed. "Mama, it's not like that. I'm not selling any drugs. I'm just—"

"Eating the fruit from the poisonous tree."

"No...I mean..."

"Did I tell you that your father was a pimp?" She paused. "Had a whole line of women. From white to black and everything in between. Now he saw a lot of money."

"What?" I frowned. "No...you never said nothing about that."

"Because I'm embarrassed. That's where he found me."

My stomach rumbled. "Mama, you were a..."

"Whore...hoe...lady of the night. A prostitute's name by any other is still the same." She sighed. "I sold my body for money and fell in love with your father in the process. Everybody told me he would never leave the game for me, despite the lies he told me regularly. And I believed him."

"Did he?"

"What you think? You see him around?" She laughed. "The money was too good and your father didn't have no skill set. Come to think of it I didn't either." She sighed. "So he was kept in a cycle that he couldn't get out of but I wasn't about to birth my children into that world."

"It's not gonna be like that with me, mama." I promised. "I'm going to school."

"Oh, baby, I really hope you telling the truth. I really hope you realize that whatever comes fast, goes away faster. Now I like Russo, I really do and that's part of my dilemma. I see the way he looks at you when he comes over for dinner. The boy is definitely in love. But a man should be an uplifting force in your life. He should never bring you to the depths he's in, especially if it's hell. And I fear if ya'll stay together that's exactly what's gonna happen."

"Nah, Russo gonna get out the game, mama." I smiled. "I know he is."

"Did he tell you that?"

"What? I mean...not really but he knows I can't be involved with all that?"

"Are you sure?" She laughed. "Don't get me wrong, the changes look good on you but in less than four months you turned into a star. Hair running down your back even though I begged you to leave it natural, makeup with the most expensive cosmetics and so many shoes I haven't seen you in the same pair twice." She paused. "So you tell me, how can a girl who has everything give it all up to start again from the bottom?"

"Mama, I...I mean..." I moved uneasily in my seat. She had backed me in a corner.

"You don't have to say anything. Besides, any words leaving your mouth are gonna be temporary and based in lies. In your heart right now you probably have all intentions on doing the right thing. But once that man wraps his arms around you it'll be all forgotten. The words of your mama won't stand a chance. Besides, you're about to be eighteen in some weeks and I can't stop you." She stood up. "Just so you know, you broke my heart."

When I got upstairs I tossed my bags on the floor in my room and looked out ahead. Maybe mama was right. I wasn't gonna give him up. I had plans to register to the local college to take my computer courses but I wanted to spend all the time I could with Russo before he left.

When my phone rang I answered it quickly. "Hello."

"Hey...you feel like talking?"

I frowned. "Who this? Jordan?"

"Yeah."

"Nigga...do me a favor. Lose my fuckin' number. You a clown."

I slammed the phone down and walked to my bags. I removed all of the clothes from one bag and moved to the next wear I saw a box wrapped in pretty blood red wrapping paper. When I opened it up it was an iPhone.

"Oh my God!" I turned it on and it was charged up. I immediately called Russo. "Baby, you got me a new phone?"

"Should've been done that." He said. "But I wanted to make sure you were mine before I gave you a cell." He laughed. "Couldn't have you calling other niggas and shit now could I?"

I laughed. "I love you so much."

"But look...you went through the other—"

"Hold up, baby, something fell out of my other bag and..." When I reached down I saw a gun and stumbled backwards. "What...what..."

"Baby girl, I know you just found that but don't worry. It's just—"

"You put a gun in my bag?" I walked to my bedroom door and closed it. "Without telling me? Russo, are you crazy?"

"I had to, Amina. The man that came over was a cop and—"

"Wait, is that the gun that was used to kill that man in the alley?" I paused. "Please don't tell me you did me like that, Russo."

"Now why would you ask me that when you really don't wanna know?"

"Russo...this is...so fucked up." I flopped on the edge of the bed. "You...you put a gun in my bag. What if the cops pulled me over? Did you not even care?"

"I wasn't thinking." He exhaled. "You right and I'm so sorry. Let me come scoop you and go get something to eat. I can make it up to you if you give me a chance."

"That's not gonna work this time."

"Amina, let's not do this again. The fighting and breaking up. You know I'm leaving soon. Why you gotta make our last days fucked up?"

"Just lose my number, Russo."

"Wait, who you talking to like that?"

"It's over!" I ended the call, tossed the phone on my bed and cried.

CHAPTER TWENTY

TAMIKA

TWO WEEKS LATER

*I*t was a cool fall day as Tamika and Reggie lie on a quilt in the backyard of the house. Looking up at the ice blue sky she rolled over to face him. "I was raped. And I'm ready to talk about it with you."

He slowly turned his head in her direction. "Wow, 'Mika. I...I...I'm sorry."

She sighed. "I guess because I'm young he...it's all dumb but he...he lured me in a van and raped me."

He pulled her to him and her head lay on his chest. "That explains a lot of stuff." He stroked her hair. "Did they catch him? Please say they did."

"No." She placed her hand on his stomach and played with one of the buttons on his blue plaid shirt. "I don't think they ever will. I haven't given them any description."

"I really wish you would." He sighed. "Is there anything I can do?"

"No...I'm better now that you here." She looked up at him. "Guess if I had to pick something it would be not to leave me."

"I have to tell you something, Tamika."

She looked at him and sat up. He did the same and they were facing each other. "You scaring me now."

He placed his hand on hers. "Don't be scared around me. Ever."

"Then why do I feel like whatever you're about to say is extra bad? Like its gonna change us?"

He sighed. "Russo got some things to do in New York in a few weeks and I'm going with him."

"But...but...what about us? What about you telling me you would never leave and stuff like that? I need you here, Reggie!"

"I'm not going forever, Tamika. Just helping Russo out with a few things."

"So that's why you been having a lot of money and dressing different?" Her brows lowered. "Because you a drug dealer now?"

"That's not fair, 'Mika. You been different too. Where you get this dress from? I know for a fact Russo been taking care of the family. Well that's my job to take care of you."

By KIM MEDINA

Tears rolled down her face. "I can't let you leave right now. I don't know how to be without you. Please."

"I got to, Tamika." He paused. "I promised."

"So the promise you made to him trumps the promise you made to me?"

She stood up and he stood up too. "Mika, being with you made me realize that life was happening around me. And while I was waiting here for my mother to come back or to find her, I should be offering more too you."

"More to me how?" She pointed at herself. "What you think I want that I don't have with you?"

He shrugged. "I don't know. But before you came into the picture I was on my ass and now I gotta chance to...make a little money and give you a life."

"If you go with him it's over."

His eyes widened. "You don't mean that."

"I do."

He shook his head rapidly, trying to erase the words he hoped never to hear from her lips again. "You don't mean that, 'Mika. Take it back."

She shook her head and ran in the house, slamming the door behind herself.

AMINA

I was sitting in my car on the side of the highway with the iPhone pressed against my ear, trying to understand what I just heard from my baby sister. She called me hysterical, which was a phone call I hated to get because it reminded me of when she was raped. And now I was trying to ask my ex-boyfriend why was he trying to hurt my family.

"Russo, why you doing this? If you wanna go to New York, just do you. Don't take Reggie too. That's foul."

He sighed and his voice sounded like he had an attitude. But I didn't care. I wanted answers and I wanted him to give them to me. "I needed somebody I trusted to go with me. Unfortunately that's him."

I slapped the steering wheel. "What's so fucking important that you need to ruin my sister's relationship though? Are you doing this just to get back at me?"

"How you sound?"

By KIM MEDINA

"How else can I sound?"

"Nah, I'm not in the business of hurting people I love. But it's funny how I been hitting your phone for weeks and you didn't pick up once." He paused. "And now you calling me about some business shit that don't have nothing to do with you? To be honest I'm not even understanding why I'm discussing any of this over the waves in the first place."

"Please don't take him with you, Russo. I can't see how you would spend all this time in the business and can't find another friend to go."

"You wild, Amina. And way out of line too."

"Well, let me be all that." I said. "My sister is in the house right now crying her eyes out. I didn't want to tell you but she was raped before we moved out here. It was a real bad situation and this is only making it worse."

"Whoa, bae." He paused. "Why you ain't tell me before? Do you know who the nigga is? I can rectify that right now."

I flopped back in the seat. "Because it wasn't my place to say anything. It still ain't my place now but what can I do?"

"Listen, this is a life and death situation. And before you ask me what that means, just remember that you were the main one saying you didn't want to know anything about my world. All I can say is this, I promise not to keep him long." He paused. "Now can we stop all this and get back to us? I miss you. And I know you gotta miss me too."

I ended the call and tossed the phone in the seat.

Please don't let nothing else happen in my family. 'Cause I can't take much more.

CHAPTER TWENTY-ONE

AMINA

I was tired after helping my sister and mother put the finishing touches on the basement. Now the house was completely restored and looked brand new in the inside, we were working on the outside over the next few days. Wesley was true to his word and wouldn't accept any money but my mother believed he would ask for his payment in some form or another, and she believed it would be more expensive than we could afford.

My mother left for work even though she could barely stand up from being so tired and Tamika went to her room, still sad about Reggie leaving with Russo. Reggie had been by everyday along with Russo but neither one of us wanted to talk to them.

I was about to walk into my room to grab my clothes for a shower when I heard something bang in Drillo's room. Afraid, I rushed toward his door and pushed it open. Drillo was on the floor, picking himself up.

I laughed at first until I saw his eyes. They were rolling around in his head. "Drillo, what you in here drinking?"

His eyes couldn't even stay on me he was so gone. "What...what you..."

Suddenly he passed out.

TAMIKA

Tamika, Amina and Pam sat in the living room looking out into space. Drillo, the youngest member of their family was on heroin and they never saw it coming.

"We lost one in the confusion of it all," Pam said, mainly to herself. "We were so caught up in getting this house together that now I—"

"Mama, this isn't your fault."

"Whose fault is it then, Amina?" She paused. "We all help each other but at the end of the day I'm responsible for every one of you. And that's real." She sat back. "I mean, I don't even know how this could've gotten started."

By KIM MEDINA

"Maybe it's his friends he doesn't want us to meet." Tamika said softly. "Who knows?"

"I'm sure it is, baby." Pam sighed. "But even if I put the blame on them it won't bring him through what he has to go through. I dealt with a heroin addiction as a teenager and it's a heavy period in a person's life. He'll be changed forever. I have to pray hard but I don't know if I have the strength."

"I'm gonna go get some air," Tamika said as she got up and walked out the backdoor.

Once outside she sat on the lawn chair and looked out into the opening. Winter was nearing so the breeze was a little cooler than it had been but Tamika didn't mind. All she wanted was some time to think about why their family constantly went through dark moments.

"Are you okay?" Reggie asked stepping up to the fence on his side of the yard.

"Like you would care," she said softly, crossing her arms over her chest.

He hopped over the fence, grabbed a chair and sat next to her. "Maybe one day you'll let me be a friend, despite what you feel right now. I would really like it if you did because I have to stay in your life."

She laughed. "So now you want to be my friend? What kind of sick shit is that?"

"Tamika, I love you. You know that I do but you won't let me in. You charging my reasons for wanting to go with Russo against how I feel about you. When the real reason I'm doing this is for us."

"Drillo's on heroin." She looked over at him. "Did you hear what I said? My little brother is on heroin and we don't know what to do with him."

Reggie looked away from her, sat back in the chair and sighed. "Whoa...I'm...I'm so sorry, 'Mika."

"If you're really sorry then stay. Please, Reggggie!"

He shook his head. "My mother was married after my father. I didn't like her new husband that much but when I look back on it, he may not have done father things with me but he was always there. My mother started experiencing some sadness I guess from my little sister running away from home and so she stopped wanting him to go to work."

"What's the point of this?"

"Just hear me out." He touched her hand. "Try to have an open mind. Please."

"Go 'head."

By KIM MEDINA

"So he would call off one day of work and then two. After that he found out she was using drugs. And then he started staying home to help her get off of them." He laughed. "That's when things got worse. Later that turned into him having an addiction and both of them started using hard."

"I'm sorry," she whispered.

"It's not your fault. I'm finding out that it's not anybody's fault. What I got from it though was two things. First, sometimes you gotta do the hard things even if it hurts someone you love." He paused. "He knew calling off work was the wrong thing to do since he had a family, but he allowed the woman he was dealing with to bring him down when she needed him to lift her up. Secondly, I learned that this drug shit was not taking anything else from me. The way I see it is, it owes me."

"How?"

"'Mika, the drug game ain't going nowhere. The money ceased in drug crimes is recycled through police departments. Even they make it legal. That's why some of the most heavy crime areas got the most money to spend in police. I look at it the same way. I mean, ain't it time for some of this drug money to be recycled to me?"

"Don't go, Reggie." Tears rolled down her face. "Please."

He stood up and exhaled. Already since the time she saw him he changed and was growing into a man before her eyes. It wasn't just about the money or the new clothes he sported. But his demeanor said so much more.

"Where's Drillo?"

"Upstairs, in his room."

He nodded. "I'll be by later to check on him." He reached into his pocket and pulled out fifty dollars. "Buy something to eat around 5:00 pm so your mama won't have to cook tonight. I'll be back by then."

"Are you leaving or not?"

"I think you already know the answer to that." He lowered his body, kissed her on the lips and hopped over the fence.

By KIM MEDINA

CHAPTER TWENTY-TWO

AMINA

Tamika and me were walking up the street from catching the school bus when she said she had to ask me something. My mind was still on Drillo and what he must be going through, and when I wasn't thinking about my brother, I was missing Russo. He had been sending flowers and money to the house but I was serious about not dealing with him anymore. It didn't mean I didn't miss him, and want him in my life, but what could I do?

"Have you had sex before?" Tamika asked me. "Like, with Jordon or Russo?"

I coughed out some of the coke I was drinking. "Uh, I'm not sure I should be answering a question about sex from my baby sister." I laughed. "Your mind shouldn't be on that anyway. Trust me, you ain't missing nothing."

"But I wanna know for a reason. I mean, I did it a few times when we were in DC, before that thing happened to me in the van and now..." She shrugged. "Now I don't know if I can do it again without thinking about being raped. The bad

THE HOUSE THAT CRACK BUILT   181

dreams don't come as much as they used to since Reggie's been around but they still there."

I nodded and then remembered what she was trying to say. She probably wanted to go all the way with Reggie but wanted to know what I was thinking first. "Did I ever tell you about the creepy man who picked me up when we were staying at that motel for a while? He was driving a Benz."

"No." She shook her head. "What happened?"

"Well he picked me up and said he was gonna take me to get something to eat. I kinda wanted to go somewhere because I was tired of dealing with...you know...everything."

"You mean me?" She asked with sad eyes.

I stopped walking and held her hand before letting it go. "I'm sorry about all that, Tamika. I do love you."

"Yeah, you used to say some pretty mean things to me when I stopped talking."

"I know and I'm realizing it wasn't right. But, I was just going through so much." I sighed. "Maybe mama was right, I was being selfish but I didn't mean any of the things I said to you. You my baby sis."

"I know." She nodded and we both started walking again. "Finish your story."

"Before I got in the car, something told me not to and I did it anyway." I looked over at her. "And I don't know what you were about to ask me but I think I do. When you with a boy next time, listen to the quiet voice. If it feels right do it and if it doesn't..." I shrugged.

"I get it."

"Why you asking?"

"You think if I did it with Reggie he'll stay?"

"Reggie pressing you out like that?" I was disappointed because I liked him so much. Tamika did way better with her first boyfriend than I ever did with mine.

"No...I mean...I want him to stay and I'm hoping it will." Tamika looked past me at the house. "Hold up, don't you know them girls?"

When I followed her pointing finger I saw Chestnut, Gucci and Yolanda standing across the street from our house and my heart pumped.

"Tamika, I need you to run in the house right away."

"No!" She yelled. "What you 'bout to do?"

"Just go okay? And lock the doors unless you see it's me."

Tamika took off running and I walked toward the house slowly. If I hurried up maybe I could call the police and stop whatever craziness was about to happen. I managed to make it to my front lawn but Chestnut was right up on me.

"So where's your little car?" She asked looking up the street. "Did he take it from you already?"

"No, I gave it back." I said looking behind me to make sure Tamika was gone. She was. "Now what do you want from me?"

"So you still messing with Russo after I told you he was my boyfriend?"

"Chestnut, I don't deal with him no more." Gucci and Yolanda walked behind me and one of them knocked my book bag off my back. I picked it up and held it in front of me. "Plus I didn't know he was your boyfriend."

"I know I told you he was my man," she said. "So you gonna lie to my face? What you think I'm stupid?"

"Chestnut, look, me and Russo is over!" I yelled. "So if you want him shoot your shot and leave me out of it." I walked away from her and Gucci punched me in my face. When I fell to the ground Gucci started kicking me in my head.

By KIM MEDINA

From where I stood it looked like Yolanda had run away but that didn't stop Gucci and Chestnut from punching and kicking me like they hated me so much. And then I felt something cool on my arm and realized for the second time in my life I had been stabbed. Except this time I wasn't going to let them put me in the hospital. I was going to fight back no matter what.

Lying on my yard, I dug into my book bag, pulled out my gun and shot Chestnut in the chest. Blood splattered everywhere and Gucci took off running down the street. I could smell a sulfur odor in the air and my body trembled and Chestnut moaned before getting quiet.

Not knowing what to do, but then remembering when my aunt fought my neighbors, I removed my key from my pocket, opened the door and dragged Chestnut inside. My aunt said the cops won't be so hard on you if you kill somebody who came into your house to do you harm. I hope she was telling the truth.

"What now?"

CHAPTER TWENTY-THREE

AMINA

I was watching Russo pay someone driving the van that just hauled off Chestnut's body thinking wow...I just killed someone. Tamika and Reggie were in the house watching TV and I was standing in the doorway of our house. When he was done the van pulled off and he walked up to me.

"It's taken care of," he paused. "And don't worry about Yolanda and Gucci. I already had a conversation with them. A firm one and they know I'm not playing." He paused. "Can I talk to you for a minute out here?"

I nodded and walked outside. "Thank you again, Russo. For doing that."

"I thought you told me you lost the gun." He whispered. "That you threw it away?"

I nodded again. "I was going to but, Chestnut and them had been threatening me and I figured it was better to have something than nothing. I didn't think I would shoot it though. Just wave it around and scare them." I shrugged. "I'm sorry."

"You never pull a gun you don't plan on shooting." He shook his head. "Bae, that gun had bodies on it."

I frowned. "So why you give it to me?"

"I didn't give it to you." He said firmly, pointing at the ground. "I hid it in your clothes until I dealt with that cop. You told me you got rid of it when I said I was coming to stash it."

I shrugged. "It happens."

"Don't tell me it happens." He said angrily. If you would've gotten locked up I would've felt like it was all my fault."

I folded my arms over my chest because actually it was. Had he never put it in my bag I wouldn't be in this situation. "I'm sorry, Russo. But you got the gun now. And like I said, I appreciate you doing that because..." I broke down crying and sat on the step. He sat next to me before gripping me in a side hug.

"Amina, I love you. I ain't never felt like this for a female before and to be honest, didn't even think it was possible. But that's the situation I'm in right now and I wouldn't take nothing from our past."

"Russo, what's this about?"

"Us." He stared into my eyes. "Look, at the end of the day I move weight. I know you not feeling it, and the situation got you wanting to leave me but I love you. And you love me. So why you letting something like the dope game drive us apart?"

"I just...I mean..."

"I wanna be with you, Amina. On my mother's heart I do, but you got to make a decision right now. If you want to be with me and want to see where we can take this thing tell me now. If not, I'm out. Just like you don't want somebody you feeling judging you for your past, I don't need people judging me where I am right now. Especially when I love the person."

I shook my head and looked away from him, the cool breeze caressing my face.

"So what's it gonna be, Amina?"

I looked at him, kissed his lips and walked in the house. I looked out the window and for a second he remained on the steps looking out ahead of him, then he got up, eased into his car and pulled off.

I went upstairs and cried.

By *KIM MEDINA*

TAMIKA

Tamika and Reggie were watching TV when he looked over at her with a smile on his face. "What you happy about?" She paused. "Because for real I don't even know why I let you come over here."

He chuckled. "Let me come over? How you sound?"

"I'm serious. You leaving and for New York and—"

"I'm not." He paused. "You won."

She sat up and looked at him, her eyes wide with excitement. "What...what made you change your mind?"

"I don't want to have to worry about 'nother nigga coming into the picture in the few months I was out." He paused. "Plus I talked to Russo about it and he worked out some other things. Got some other people to help. I think he wants me to be here too."

"Some other things?"

He nodded. "Listen, I'm serious about feeling like the game owes me. And Russo directing it for

THE HOUSE THAT CRACK BUILT   189

me. And I'm not telling you I'm out the game. What I can promise is that I won't let it keep me as long as some niggas."

She looked away and he moved her chin so that their eyes met again.

"Can you get with that?"

She nodded and kissed him passionately. They were still embraced when there was a knock at the door. He got up, answered it and looked behind him back at Tamika. It was somebody for him. "Give me a sec." He said before walking outside, closing the door behind himself.

Curious, Tamika walked to the window and saw him talking to a man who looked hard on his luck but was holding some crumpled money, which he was giving to him. Tamika's stomach rumbled as she realized he was a drug addict and her lovable boyfriend Reggie was serving him. But what could she do. She had already made a decision that she was going to ride for hers no matter the consequences.

And then her world was rocked. Hard.

When she turned her head and saw the news come on, she dropped where she stood when she saw the man whose face appeared across the screen. From the low volume she could see that he

By KIM MEDINA

was being arrested for raping and murdering a young girl. Something she had been through herself.

The door opened and Reggie walked in, shocked to see her on the floor. "What happened?" He asked rushing to her, helping her up. "Are you okay?"

She pointed at the screen. "It was him. He raped me."

Reggie looked at the TV and frowned. His face filled with rage lines Tamika didn't know he was capable of making. His chest moving up and down rapidly. Up until that moment he had always been her little angel but now she saw not only did he love her beyond all else, but also that he was capable of the worst if someone hurt her again.

Murder.

The newscaster went on to explain that Chris Mike, a cop and resident of Philadelphia, would make repeated visits to D.C. to rape young women. He felt he could get away with it if he was away from his town and he was right, until he came in line with Melanie Connor, a fifteen-year-old young boxer who beat him into a coma after fighting for her life.

After he regained consciousness, he was charged with the murder of another young girl and the rape of twenty. A number scattered across the bottom of the screen indicating that if anyone knew anything else about the crime or was assaulted that they should come forward.

He helped her to the sofa. "You gonna contact them, 'Mika?"

She shook her head no and looked at him. "Up until this moment I couldn't breathe on a regular because I didn't feel safe. Now I got you and we working on helping my brother through what he going through. That man will not take another day of my life. For now that's all I need. " She hugged him tightly.

By KIM MEDINA

CHAPTER TWENTY-FOUR

AMINA

Russo and me were sitting in a diner off Route 40 in Ellicott City eating breakfast. The day I didn't want to happen came. I mean, I knew the day would come when Russo would finally leave but to be honest I thought he would have left a long time ago. Or would change his mind and stay.

After we ate, he reached in his pocket and handed me a stack of money. "Put that up. Use it for whatever you need."

I looked at it and stuffed it inside my purse. "Thank you." He paused. "So there ain't no way I can get you to change your mind?"

"Amina, come on." He nodded and scratched between the rows of his braids. "You know, I know why you doing this and as fucked up as it is I understand it."

"What you talking about?"

"You figured if you'd break up with me then it wouldn't hurt so bad when I left." He paused. "So is it working?"

I smiled. "No...not at all."

"That's 'cause you belong to a trap nigga."

I shook my head. "But that can't be my life."

"You already took a life." He whispered. "You did the worst. What's a little coke?"

"I'm trying to forget that part." I looked around. "I'm talking about Chestnut."

"Well I told you I wouldn't ask again and I mean it. I don't ever want you to feel like I made you do something you didn't want to by being with me."

"Well maybe I was wrong." I said softly.

He smiled brightly. "Wait...what was that again?" He laughed. "Because I need to hear this forever. You don't understand, I been envisioning you say you want me again."

I nodded and took a deep breath. "I don't know what being with you means for me but...I mean...I really wanna try. If you still want me in your life."

He reached across the table and placed his hands overtop of mine. "Then lets not play anymore games with each other. I want to spoil you and —"

"Russo, I thought you were in New York!" A girl with a long black weave said stepping up to us. She was carrying a brown Louis Vuitton

194   *By KIM MEDINA*

purse and was so pretty she made me feel smaller. Insignificant.

"Tamara, I'm holding a conversation with—"

"Nigga, don't tell me what to do! You fuck me and then you do me like this?"

My heart was instantly broken. I stood up and said, "I'm...I'm...out of here."

"Then leave, bitch!" She yelled.

All of a sudden two men across the diner rushed up to us, and grabbed her, lifting her off her feet. At first I thought they were security until Russo gave them orders. That told me that he always had people following him and I didn't know. The girl was screaming and cursing as they dragged her out the door.

Tears rolled down my face. "Russo, I thought you loved me. And wanted to be with me."

"I do, Amina." He said. "I fucked that bitch when you kept telling me it was over." He shrugged. "I mean, what you wanted me to do?"

"To love me!" I yelled. "And to do right by me! You know my heart was broken before and...you know what." I stopped and threw my hands up because it was useless. "It's my turn to go watch Drillo. This right here...I don't have time for."

"Then let me go with you."

"It's over! And I take back everything I said about wanting to be with you." I stormed out.

Me, Reggie and Tamika were standing by Drillo's bedside. He had overdosed again when mama stepped out to go grocery shopping, something I said I would do. Instead, I let Russo talk me into seeing him at the diner and all I got was my feelings hurt and embarrassed.

Drillo looked so badly as he lay unconsciously, tubes connected to his body.

"You think he gonna die?" Tamika asked as Reggie held onto her hand. They were seated on the right side of his bed, me on the left.

"Don't talk like that, 'Mika," Reggie said. "Only positivity right now."

"But how can we be positive when—"

Suddenly Drillo's eyes opened and we all stood up and walked to the bed. "Where's ma?" He asked in a whisper.

"She not feeling too good," I said touching his hand. "She'll come by later when she is though."

By KIM MEDINA

The truth was mama felt so guilty about leaving Drillo that she had a migraine headache so bad, it put her to her knees. She tried to come but I begged her to stay, saying it would make him feel worse.

"I gotta tell you something," he said to me. "Alone."

I nodded at Reggie and Tamika and they walked out. "What's up?"

"I was the one who put Mrs. Connelly's phone in your bedroom."

My eyes widened. "What...but why? And how?"

"Wesley gave it to me. He was in on it with Chestnut and them I think." He paused. "I think he was mad at how you treated him or something. I'm...I'm sorry."

I couldn't even be mad at him because I was more concerned about him getting better. Still, things were starting to make sense. "Don't worry about it, Drillo."

"Do gay people go to hell?"

My eyebrows rose. "Mama says ain't no hell 'cept for the one people put themselves in here on earth. She said God is all love and would never give a bad person a hell to run and make people suffer."

"But if there is a hell do you think gay people would be in it?" He continued.

My heart rocked. Was he saying what I think he was? "Drillo, of course not. Why you even say that?"

He looked away. "Well...I kind of did some things with Wesley. Things I liked at first and then...then I felt bad for. He told me he used to feel bad too when he did it with his uncles but if I used drugs I would feel better. It worked at first but even with the drugs the thoughts started not to leave. So I did more."

My legs felt weak and I flopped in the sofa. "So...Wesley was raping you?"

"No...I mean...I don't think so but—"

"Drillo you still a kid. And whatever he did to you, even if you think you liked it at first, still makes it his fault." I squeezed his hand harder. "Is this why you been drinking and stuff?"

"Yeah."

"But you were doing that before we met Wesley."

He nodded. "I been feeling this way for a minute. I'm talking about being gay." He paused. "But please, don't tell mama and don't tell nobody. I don't want Wesley being mad at me."

By KIM MEDINA

"Drillo, I can't promise that."

"Don't tell mama! Or Tamika or Reggie!" He yelled, causing the beeping heart machine to speed up.

"Okay, okay," I whispered trying to calm him down. The machines grew quieter. "I won't say a word to them. You just get better. We got a lot of stuff to do." I grabbed my purse and walked toward the door.

And I knew exactly where I was going.

To the police.

CHAPTER TWENTY-FIVE

AMINA

I was in the bed taking a nap when my head started pounding and jolted me out of my sleep. I placed my warm hand over my clammy head and prayed that the thumping would go away. The pain was so harsh that I could barely see and I felt dizzy even though I was still in bed. I never thought migraines were hereditary but lately I had been getting as much as mama if not more.

Wanting to grab some of mama's medicine, I got out of bed, slid into my grey sweatpants and then walked to the window. A light amount of snow was falling down and it was so pretty. Winter was definitely here.

I realized how much better it would be to look at if Russo and me were still together. I thought about him so much that sometimes I didn't know if I could stand living without him. Just thinking about him not being in my life made me feel bad but it was true.

Instead of being with the one person who I thought loved me back I was alone, left to think of

By KIM MEDINA

the awful things Wesley had done to my kid brother, who was being kept for observation at the hospital. True to her word, Mama went down there when she was feeling better to try and talk some sense into them but they were adamant that he was not well and so they couldn't let him go, believing he was suicidal.

Although I didn't tell ma or Tamika, I did go to the police the same day. At first they acted as if they didn't believe me but then another officer walked in and he looked like he was no nonsense. The moment I said Wesley's name he asked if he had a brother name Peter and from that point he got involved.

When I asked what would be done, he told me to let him handle it and that this would be the nail in Wesley and Peter's coffin. I kept telling him that Peter didn't have anything to do with it but he said he's more involved than I realized. And that both brothers raped many in their day, and got away with it.

When I walked back over to the bed to put my socks on, Reggie knocked on the door. It was open and he hung by the doorway. "I just ordered some chicken cheese subs. You hungry?"

"They already here?" I asked with raised brows.

"Yeah, but you know how I do it. I get a few extras in case anybody want one. Your mother said no and Tamika already on her second."

"On her second?" I repeated. "See you 'bout to make my sister extra fat."

"Good, that way nobody will want her but me." He laughed and then walked further inside, sitting next to me. "How you feeling? I mean really?"

"Please don't tell me you in here about Russo."

"If I said yes would you be mad?"

I rolled my eyes. "Reggie, he was with another girl while we were—"

"Broken up," he said finishing my sentence. "And I wouldn't be saying any of this to you because it's not my style. But Russo been prop'd a few times by different females and he never went at them, until he came by that day when ya'll were sitting on the steps, and he said he would never ask you to get back together again."

"You don't know what you talking about."

"You probably right. I'm not with yah every second of the day." He nodded. "But what if I am? What if you 'bout to let the one nigga for you get

By KIM MEDINA

away on account of a misunderstanding?" He stood up. "I'ma leave you too it." He was about to walk out when he turned around and said, "And I put the subs in the oven on low in case you want one. I'll cut it off in a few minutes so they won't get hard."

"AMINA!" My sister yelled from inside the house.

Her cries must've startled Reggie too because we both ran to her room thinking she was there. When we didn't see her we heard her yell again. "REGGIE, COME NOW!"

I rushed down the steps only to feel the cool air on my body. The door was wide open and Peter was inside, grabbing our sofa and pulling it toward the exit. "What are you doing?" I yelled. "And why you got the door open? You letting the heat out!"

"My nigga, don't touch none of this shit," Reggie yelled stepping in front of him.

"Why are you doing this?" I asked Peter.

"Because you have to go!" He yelled. "This was only a month to month lease and now it's up."

"But I thought we could stay here as long as we fixed the house up. I thought you told my mother that was the deal."

"I can do whatever I want, this is my house!" He went to grab the sofa again and Reggie shoved him backwards.

"I done already told you not to touch nothing else in here!" Reggie yelled. "Ain't you listening?"

"Well if you have that attitude then maybe I'll call the police. Like you did, Amina. And it didn't work because they were all lies!" He removed his cell phone when all of a sudden I heard my mother's voice behind me.

"What's going on?" She asked at the top of the steps, her red robe flying by her feet do to the door being open and the wind rushing in, rearranging everything not bolted down.

"Mama, we got it." I said. "Just go back upstairs." She wasn't well and I didn't want her getting more upset.

"Don't lie to your mother. I'm throwing you out on the streets." Peter continued.

"What? Why? I...I..." My mother pressed her hand over her heart and her eyes widened.

Suddenly she fell down the steps and gripped her chest as she lay on the floor.

"MAMA!" I yelled rushing toward her. My world would come crashing down if something happened to my mother. Who would love me like

204 *By KIM MEDINA*

she does? Who would care about my well-being, and who would fight the world to see that our family stayed together? Not having my mother just wasn't an option at anytime in my life.

"Call the ambulance!" I yelled.

"I'm already on it," Reggie said with one hand on the phone and the other arm around my sister who was crying uncontrollably.

When I looked at the doorway Peter was still staring at us. But it was the person behind him that made sense out of everything. Wesley stood next to his car, arms crossed over his chest and a hateful look on his face. He was probably moving in the house, which is why he helped us fix it up all along. He was also probably the one who beat him up.

I was sure now that this wasn't about anything other than him raping my brother and being mad that I told the police.

I had to think of our next move but first, I had to help my mother..

CHAPTER TWENTY-SIX

AMINA

Mama's hospital room was very warm, cozy and filled with beautiful flowers. The doctor said he wanted it comfortable for her because her bones ached and she refused to take around the clock medicine for pain. She had a heart attack, something she had been having regularly but never told us until it was too late.

Me, Reggie and Tamika were there watching *Family Feud* with her until she grabbed the remote and turned it off. I got up and walked to her bedside. Tamika and Reggie remained seated but looked at us. "You okay, mama?" I smiled. "You want me to tell the doctor to make it warmer?"

She touched my hand. "No, I'm fine." She seemed so much at peace. "You know, I'm proud of you."

"Mama, you don't have to say—"

"Just listen, sweetheart." Her voice was barely above a whisper but I understood everything. "I'm proud of you because you've come around quicker than I could've imagined. And I know you

By KIM MEDINA

don't see the strength in yourself but its there. It's always been there." She paused. "And I can see you are battling in your heart on what to do about your relationship with Russo."

"Mama, I'm over it." I gripped her hand. "Trust me. I just want you to be okay."

"I know you feel it in your heart but the journey is long, Amina. The only thing that makes the load easier is family. And being with someone who cares about you as much as you do them. And I think you found that in Russo. But be careful not to lose yourself in him." She turned her head and reached for Tamika. "Come here."

Tamika walked over to her, tears rolling down her cheeks. "Yes, mama?"

"I want you to know that what you went through that day was not your fault."

"But I—"

Mama placed her hand up. "Just listen to me." She paused. "Mothers are supposed to protect their children and give them the tools necessary to know when danger is present. And I failed you." She wiped the tears rolling down her eyes. "But, baby the strength you possess is something that I marvel at everyday. Not only did you pull yourself up, but you pushed yourself to lead a full life and nobody can take that away from you. Ever. Since you've overcome this you can overcome everything."

"Mama, I'm scared."

"Don't be." She squeezed her hand. "I don't mean to make you scared." She grabbed my hand too. "I just want you both to remember how important you are to one another. Sometimes things may get scattered and you may fight, but you must always come back to each other. Because this is your foundation, and it cannot be broken. Do you understand?"

"Yes, mama," I said.

"We will," Tamika responded.

"Now leave me a little while." She paused. "I want to talk to Reggie."

PAM

When Amina and Tamika left the room Reggie walked up to Pam slowly. "Yes, ma'am?" He was nervous and didn't know whether to look into her eyes or on the floor. She exuded everything his

208   *By KIM MEDINA*

mother was before the system took her and in her presence he was filled with automatic respect and admiration.

"Tamika told me a little about your past." She paused. "And I know a little about your future." She said sternly.

"Ma'am, I just be—"

"I saw you transition from a young man who had fallen on hard times, to a young man who has embraced the curse of the streets by selling drugs. And I'm not here to judge you."

Guilt weighed down his head and he looked at the floor. "I'm sorry. I didn't know what else to do."

"Son, you are a king. Don't you ever utter the words I'm sorry. Your mother left you in an impossible position and since you had no skills, your future was limited." She paused. "But I'm telling you that it's not too late. You can still become something other than what society believes you to be. A drug dealer. I'm not here to say you should do this or do that, but what I would like to ask of you is to be there for my family. They gonna need you now more than ever."

His forehead wrinkled. "Why...what's going on?"

Pam's eyes grew heavier as the Holy Spirit relaxed her achy body to take her home. "I'm not gonna make it, son and my girls aren't going to be able to deal with this alone. This is why I need you to be from the streets but not of them. There's a difference."

Tears rolled down his cheeks and she placed her hand on top of his. "I...I'll try."

"That's all I can ask." She paused, her breaths becoming harder to expense. "And now I want to say something to you as if I were your mother, in her right frame of mind." She paused. "Reggie, I'm sorry for abandoning you. I'm sorry for shaking my responsibility as a mother. But I want you to know that I love you and that my faults do not need to rest upon your head. Be strong. Be the son, man, husband, father and leader I know you can be."

Reggie was crying so hard he was on his knees, his hand still touching Pam's as he wept. Her words meant more to him than he could've ever imagined. Who knew he needed to hear the heart to heart talk as much as he did? It was evident now. It was as if she had landed on him a spell that would last him throughout the rest of his life. Except it wasn't a spell.

It was real.

By KIM MEDINA

And just like that, Pam Hartwell took her last breath.

When the machine went to flat line indicating that she passed on, Tamika and Amina busted into the room, crying so hard they rocked the hospital workers and patients who were within earshot. It didn't take everyone long to realize that the cries and pleas that landed on their ears were of the worst kind.

They belonged to children who had just lost their mother.

CHAPTER TWENTY-SEVEN

AMINA

My mother died two weeks ago, during my eighteenth birthday, and the pain didn't go anywhere. Add to that the fact that Peter threw us out of the house after her funeral last week, and we had been living in an upscale hotel in Baltimore ever since. There was no plan in sight. I don't even know how Reggie managed but he did. It seems like ever since my mother died he became this angel and father figure all together. Like she breathed life into him for us and I was so grateful.

I was lying on the bed next to Amina while Drillo was in the other bed taking a nap. We still managed to watch him around the clock, to make sure he wasn't using and so far it was working. That was really important to us since mama was serious about us being together and taking care of each other before she went away.

I was definitely going through the motions.

Not only was I missing the person who gave me life, but I also missed Russo. I tried to call his number to tell him my mother passed and found

By KIM MEDINA

out it was disconnected. Reggie said he hadn't heard from him either, and I started to feel like he was avoiding me on purpose. Maybe I would too after how I yelled at him at the diner.

Reggie was out getting dinner when Tamika rolled over and looked at me. I frowned because she was looking hard. "You know I hate to be stared at."

"You think we gonna be okay?"

I shrugged. "Well at least they can't tear us apart. I'm legal now. Old enough to take care of us anyway."

"So where are we gonna stay?" She paused. "You don't have a job and Reggie selling drugs. Who gonna let us live with them?"

I sighed because she was right. "I don't know what to say, Tamika." I shrugged. "A lot of stuff been happening and I'm still trying to sort it all out, you know?" I paused and looked at Drillo. "I mean I know this can't be the end to our story. We better than that."

Tamika looked back at Drillo. "I forgot to tell you something," she whispered. "Yesterday when I was in the bathroom, and you and Reggie caught and Uber to get some food, Drillo was outside."

My eyebrows rose. "Outside doing what?"

"I think he was trying to get some stuff." She paused. "Was talking to dealers but I think it didn't work because he was broke."

My heart banged into my chest. I was hoping that since mama died the rest of life would get easier. I guess that's not the case. "Why didn't you tell me?"

"Because I didn't want to bring bad news to you, Amina. We got enough of that around here."

"Well did he get anything?"

She shrugged. "Like I said, I don't think so. But for real I can't be sure."

I shook my head. "We can't have him—"

"I hear yah talking about me." Drillo said before rubbing his eyes and sitting up. "I'm not dead and yah being rude."

I looked at Tamika and we both looked at him. His hair was beady and he wouldn't let us brush it or shave it. "We know you can hear us, Drillo." I lied.

"Do you still wanna use?" Tamika asked. "Because I saw you talking to somebody the other day."

"It hurts bad, mama dying and stuff. I don't be wanting to think about it a lot and...and that

By KIM MEDINA

stuff is the only way I can feel a little better you know?"

"But that's the wrong way," Tamika said.

"How yah sound?"

I frowned. "What that mean?"

"Your ex-boyfriend sells drugs, Amina." He looked at Tamika. "And your new boyfriend is a drug dealer too. It's a real conflict of interests in the house."

"Since you throwing around big boy statements then how 'bout this one," I said, "if you get caught using again, I'm putting you back into that place. I'm not about to have you die on me and break my promise to mama."

"Me either," Tamika said. "It's just us now and...and...you know what I'm trying to say."

"Ain't nobody dying I just...I mean...I don't know." He paused. "I just want this all to go away. The pain of losing mama and...and other stuff."

I knew he meant Wesley.

The door opened and Reggie walked inside holding two large pizzas from Ledos. He placed them on the counter and walked up to us. "I got an idea." He paced a little by the bed.

"I'm listening," Tamika said.

"We should go back to the house."

"But…but they threw us out," Tamika said.

"Yeah, but it was done illegally." He paused. "I don't know what made them do it but—"

"I know why they did it," Drillo said.

"You don't have to tell them, Drillo," I said. I shook my head softly from left to right. "It's not necessary."

"Yes it is." He looked down. "I was…I mean me and…I…"

"Wesley raped you didn't he?" Reggie asked. "Wow, that nigga still a creep after all these years."

Drillo looked up at him. "Yeah…but how did you…I mean…know?"

"He tried to come at me one time." Reggie paused. "My mom had been gone a while and I needed some food and…"

"Did you?" Tamika asked, with wide eyes.

"Nah, but when you hurting as bad as I was, before I started saving up, you pray you never have to go that far. That's all you can do. That's why I didn't want Wesley around but both of you got mad at me when I brought it up. Saying you needed the house fixed up so I tried to just watch him while he was there."

By KIM MEDINA

Tamika looked at Drillo. "Why didn't you tell us?"

"Because I didn't want yah involved"

I felt guilty 'cause I knew I was the real reason everything got set off. "Well since we being honest, I kinda told the police about what you said."

Drillo's jaw hung. "What you do that for?"

"Because I didn't want him getting away with it. Or hurting someone else." I shrugged. "Call me wrong but he can't go around doing that type stuff."

Drillo looked down. "Yeah...I know."

"Me too," Tamika said.

"See this makes me want to fight even more for the house. How this nigga gonna throw yah out just because he got mad you went to the cops on account of something his brother did? He probably killed Jamie too. He used to be around him all the time."

I thought about what he was saying and realized he was right. We honored our agreement when we worked on that house, even if we used Wesley to do it. Nobody was taking the house my mother wanted us to live in, and I didn't care what we had to do.

THE HOUSE THAT CRACK BUILT   217

"You know what, Reggie's right! I say we go back and if he tries to kick us out we fight! With all we got!"

By KIM MEDINA

CHAPTER TWENTY-EIGHT

AMINA

We'd been back in the house for two days and things were quiet. Me and Reggie went grocery shopping and for both days I made a huge breakfast, lunch and dinner before we watched TV together at night. Things were going smooth and on the third day after dinner I looked over at Tamika, Drillo and Reggie and couldn't believe I was able to smile. We all thought about mama everyday but for the first time in a long time things felt normal and that made me hopeful but scared.

When there was a knock I looked at everyone and slowly stood up.

"Who you think that is?" Drillo whispered.

"I'll go find out, just stay right here."

"I'm going with you." Reggie stood up and followed me. He was right at my side when I looked out the peephole and felt as if the breath had been knocked from my body. It was the cop who thought I stole Mrs. Connelly's phone.

So what did he want now?

I opened the door and crossed my arms over my chest, just waiting for him to say we had to leave. In a few seconds in my mind, I already acted out all the ways I would tell him I wasn't going anywhere and how we had all rights to be here. "Yes? Is there something I can help you with because we busy."

"Actually there is." He paused. "I need to talk to you for a moment about a very important matter." He looked at Reggie. "In private, I hope you don't mind."

"Whatever you got to say to me he can be here to listen." I said seriously. The cold air was racking my bones and Reggie put his jacket over my shoulders.

"Well may I come in at least? We don't want the neighbors thinking you troublemakers now do we?"

"The neighbors can think whatever they want." Reggie said. "They do that anyway, so you fine out here, bruh."

"Okay then," the officer started, before removing a pen and a pad from his pocket and flipping a few pages. "I'm here about the disappearance of Chestnut Levi." I uncrossed my arms and they hung by my sides. Hearing her

By KIM MEDINA

name felt like somebody slapped me in the back of my head so hard I hit the ground face first.

"Okay. What about her?" I was trying to sound like I wasn't bothered but it was obvious that I was shook. I just hoped the cop didn't pick up on it because Reggie sure did, judging by the way he looked at me.

"She's been missing for over a month and someone said they last saw her here." He paused. "The details are a little sketchy but from what I'm told you two had a serious argument."

Reggie looked at me again before looking back at the officer. I was too stunned to speak. "Well people say a lot of things in this neighborhood." Reggie said. "You gotta be careful about what you believe. You of all people should know that."

"That may be true but Chestnut is a minor and we take missing minors very seriously. If you don't have anything to hide this should go smoothly."

I took a deep breath, slipped into my timberlands with no socks and stepped outside because I didn't want Tamika and Drillo overhearing anything. Reggie moved with me.

"Look, I don't know who told you she was last seen here but they lying and to be honest I'm not even surprised. I was never her friend and never wanted to be. She came over here to say a few things when we first moved in, but since then it's been bad."

The officer frowned and I realized I said too much. "What do you mean bad?"

"Uh...nothing...I...I mean I was dating her ex-boyfriend for awhile and she hated me because of it." I shrugged. "It wasn't as deep as what she was trying to make it out to be but we didn't like each other."

"Did you hate her enough to hurt her?"

"What...no...I..." I felt a little lightheaded because he was asking me questions I knew the answer too. What if he saw it on my face? Yes I hurt her. I even killed her but it was all in self-defense. I knew he would never understand so there was no use in me trying to explain. "No I would not hurt her. I never cared about her either which way. Just wanted her to stay away from me."

"Are you here to charge her with something?" Reggie asked.

"Who are you again?" The officer questioned.

"I'm a friend. Now can you answer my question?"

By KIM MEDINA

"We aren't here to charge anybody with anything." He put the pad back in his pocket. "But we will get down to the bottom of where she is."

"And we hope you do." Reggie said. "Now bounce. You fucking up family time." He slammed the door in his face.

"Everything okay?" Drillo asked, still sitting on the sofa with Tamika.

"Yeah...everything is fine."

"So what they want?" Tamika asked. "For us to leave?"

"Nope, and I already told yah, we not leaving no matter what anybody tells us. We in this house for the long haul. And mama would want it that way."

"Can I talk to you for a moment?" Reggie asked me.

"Uh...yeah."

"Well hurry up back," Tamika said. "We 'bout to put on the other movie."

Reggie and me walked into the kitchen, flipped on the light and stood in the middle of the floor. "What was that about?" He asked me.

"What...I mean...is the..."

"You're stuttering, 'Mina," he whispered. "Do you know something about that girl?"

"Yeah."

Reggie nodded. "Do you know something, *know something*?"

"I think you understand what I mean." I sighed. "But as far as I know Russo took care of it."

Reggie breathed a sigh of relief. "Oh...cool." He put his hand on his chest. "That makes it all better."

I frowned. "Why you so relieved now?"

"Because if Russo got involved they can look for the body until they can't look no more, they'll never find her. I just didn't want her to be buried in this house. Now all we gotta worry about is Wesley."

CHAPTER TWENTY-NINE
TAMIKA

*T*amika rolled over in her bed and looked at Reggie who was staring at her with wide eyes. "Wow, you being creepy."

He laughed. "Why I gotta be all that?"

"Because you staring at me like I'm a plate of food instead of being sleep." She lifted her head and looked at the clock. "It's four in the morning." She lay back down.

"I know...I been doing this a lot though."

She yawned and covered her mouth with her hand. "Really? Why? It ain't like I got a banging body or nothing."

He laughed. "I got a lot of reasons. I can't believe the house that took away my mother gave me you." He paused. "If somebody would've told me this I wouldn't believe them. My mother was actually getting high in here and now..." He looked around. "And now it represents you."

She smiled. "So you gonna go looking for her anytime soon?"

"Nah. Probably not."

"Why?"

"Because yah my family now. Why I gotta go out there looking for somebody who may or may not wanna be in my life? Don't seem smart to me know what I mean?"

She nodded. "My momma used to say something that she thought I wasn't listening too." Tamika smiled.

"What was it?"

She sat up Indian style and he did the same. "She said never create a goal you don't plan on finishing. Because over time not completing the goal will take little bites out of your confidence. She said a little bite here and there doesn't feel that bad but over time the little bites hurt more. And all of a sudden you wonder why you feel worthless and the whole time it's because you never finish what you started."

He nodded. "What if...what if..."

"She wants you, Reggie." She touched his face. "I want you."

"Maybe when all this blows over I'll go looking." He sighed. "Right now my place is here."

"I understand and I'm so grateful." She paused. "That's why if you want to...you know...do stuff we can. I think I'm ready to go to the next level with you."

By KIM MEDINA

He frowned. "Do stuff. Like what?"

"You know...if you want to have sex I'm okay with it."

He frowned. "Have I ever made you feel like us not having sex was an issue for me?" he paused. "Ever?"

"No...I just..."

"When we finally fuck, I don't want you having to think about what happened to you in that van. That's why I never brought it up. I definitely don't want you to have to ask me if that's something we both want. It'll just be natural, 'Mika. We got our lives ahead of us you know what I mean?"

She smiled. "Yes."

"Trust me, I'm good." She lay down and he climbed behind her in a spooning fashion. "Now I gotta come clean about something that may scare you. It may scare you a lot."

"'Go 'head."

"I'm the one who set fire to this house."

She popped up. "What...why..." she placed her hand over her chest. Her heart pounding like drums. "But...but you could never."

"I could and I did." He sat up and looked into her twinkling eyes. "I tried to burn it down, hoping it would take away the fucked up shit my mother went through. But for some reason it wouldn't ignite all the way. It was like somebody was blowing out the fire in each room. Now I'm thinking it was because if I did burn it down, I would never have found you. There would be nothing left."

She smiled slowly. "I don't know why the idea of somebody burning down a house but couldn't is the most romantic thing I ever heard in my life."

"Stick with me," he said jokingly. "Because you haven't seen nothing yet."

Amina, Drillo, Tamika and Reggie were startled when loud banging rocked the home in the early morning. They all rushed downstairs only to see that Peter had kicked the door down, right off the hinges. Behind him was a crew of men wearing moving gloves who made it clear they were there to evict them all.

"What you doing?" Amina yelled as the cold air rolled in and attacked them where they stood dressed in pajamas. Just like the day her mother

By KIM MEDINA

took to a heart attack, which made her feelings for him worse.

"I told you to leave my house and you insisted on coming back!" He yelled and then looked back at his men. "Throw them out on their asses."

"Listen, you can't do this!" Reggie said pushing Peter backwards. "You don't have any rights."

"How you gonna tell me what rights I have?" Peter questioned placing his hands on his hips. "You and your so called friends are the ones who don't have any rights to be here. Besides, I'm selling it to my brother."

"Please, our mama wanted us to be here," Tamika yelled. "Don't do this to us."

"Fuck your brother!" Amina yelled.

"Like I said, your time is—"

Suddenly loud music covered the background and cut Peter off. Everyone was distracted as six black escalades pulled up in front of the house. From the confines of the vehicle men poured, totaling thirty with Russo in the lead.

Amina smiled brightly before remembering that she was fake mad at him. She missed him so much she'd given herself ulcers, having to take Pepto Bismol most nights just to get through the days, something she hadn't told anyone.

Russo rushed up to her and said, "Bae, why you ain't tell me about your mother? I would've...I would've...."

Amina kissed him, stopping any words from flowing. It was as if they were alone and nothing else mattered. "I love you and I don't want to be without you anymore."

Russo's eyes widened. "You serious?"

She nodded rapidly. "I was trying to find you and...and your phone was disconnected. I saw what it would be like not to have you around and I can't do that, Russo. I can't."

"I'm sorry, bae. I'm a trap nigga," he said. "We gotta switch the phones out every now and again."

"So how you know what was happening?" Tamika asked with wide eyes.

He looked at Reggie. "He got in contact with a mutual friend and lets say the rest is history." Russo focused on Peter. "Now...what you gonna do first is put this door back on. Then you gonna sign over the deed to this house and put it in my girl's name."

Peter stumbled backward. "And if I don't?"

The twenty-nine men surrounded him and the movers, sending the movers back to their trucks speeding away. "Do I need to say much more? Or

230   *By KIM MEDINA*

you want me to make you feel something?" He paused. "And to make sure you stay the fuck away from my people..." he whistled and looked at one of the trucks. A window rolled down and a twenty-five-year old gay man stuck his head out.

"Hold up, that's Jamie!" Reggie said pointing at him. "I thought he was dead."

"Yeah, I know," Russo smiled looking at Peter. "Peter did too, didn't you? And you and I both know he got the tapes to everything you and your brother did to him. He was a minor when you raped him. And if they leak you'll be gone for life."

Peter turned to walk away.

"Fuck is you doing?" Russo yelled. "The door. Fix it."

Peter got to work.

Wesley pulled up in front of his house and parked. Tormented as a kid himself, he continued to act out the abuses done on him to others. His mind alternated between love and hate, with hate winning most of the time.

When he stepped out of his truck, he heard a branch crack and realized what time it was. Murder time. Five men, with Russo in front, surrounded him.

"So it ends like this for me huh?" Wesley asked. "This is my story?"

"You made this story a long time ago. I'm just writing the last chapter."

"This about what I did to you?" Wesley asked.

Russo cleared his throat and looked at his men, hoping they didn't hear him. "I don't know what you talking about, slim. You could never do anything to me. But this is for everybody else that you fucked up though. Enjoy hell." Russo walked away.

"I'll see you when you get there! Did you hear me? I'll see you when you get there!" Wesley yelled before gunfire sounded off.

Amina opened the door to the house to rush outside and grab her phone. On the way back inside she smelled perfume in the air and smiled.

By KIM MEDINA

"Hey, mama. We're okay." A calming breeze rushed over her and she walked back inside where Russo, Reggie and Drillo sat at the dinner table. Amina placed a pan of fried chicken in the middle that sat on the stove. In that moment she remembered her mother and the night her sister was found in the van. That seemed like a lifetime ago. The landscape of her life was changed but she still had a family and all intentions on making it work.

Things were way easier. Not only because of Russo but also because of the lawsuit Tamika won against the apartment complex when she was raped. Amina made her put it in her bank, promising to leave it alone.

When the chicken was on the table, she sat next to Russo and he planted a wet kiss on her lips. He loved her beyond all.

"Ew....cut all that shit out," Drillo said.

"So you just gonna cuss now 'cause ma gone?" Tamika asked.

Everybody laughed.

Things were peaceful.

For now.

EPILOGUE

TWO YEARS LATER

A mina was in the living room vacuuming when there was a firm knock at the door. After all the years she was still in the house she rebuilt with her mother. "Tamika, Reggie somebody come get it."

She was trying to clean up because later she had a birthday party for her two-year-old daughter with Russo. Their love had grown bounds and leaps and she was determined that it would last. Yes she had finally come around to accepting that he was a drug dealer. And yes she allowed him to buy her jewelry every month, a brand new Mercedes with her name on the plates that sat outside and more clothes than she could keep in her house. But With Amina there were still things she wouldn't do.

She wouldn't move into his mansion although she stayed there on the weekends. She wouldn't marry him although he asked a million times, until he got out of the game, and she was serious about finishing college as a computer programmer. Two

By KIM MEDINA

years in and she was already making strides in the right direction in honor of her mother.

She wasn't the only one making progress. Both Reggie and Tamika were finishing high school and already had full scholarships to John Hopkins for medicine, courtesy of Russo of course. Their relationship flourished and to show their commitment to each other they still hadn't had sex, even though Tamika desperately wanted to and begged him most nights. In his mind he wanted to wait until she was his wife and do right by her, something she wasn't used to in the least.

And then there was Drillo.

Unfortunately they lost him to the streets a long time ago. They hadn't seen or heard from him but every now and again the house would be broken into, and the money that they conveniently left on the table for him to steal, would be taken away. Drillo knowing how to find them was another reason Amina and the rest didn't want to move. Hope was diminished but it wasn't gone. They just couldn't put themselves at risk because Drillo ran with the cruelest of individuals in the streets.

People who knew them called their union a little weird because both sisters basically lived with their boyfriends, but to Amina their life was relatively simple, although that was about to change.

Drastically.

When no one came to the door she cut off the vacuum and stomped toward it. She didn't bother to ask who it was before pulling the door open, because she belonged to Russo and that made her off limits. In a gist she was safe.

Or was she?

On the other side of the door was a battered excuse for a woman. All of her teeth were knocked out of her mouth, her hair was completely bald with the exception of a few patches and the white dress she was wearing was covered in old blood.

And then there was the smell, which was so wretched it was as if she crawled up from hell.

"Yes?" Amina frowned.

"Your red ass must be Amina!" She said with her toothless smile. "You don't know me but I'm Reggie's mama and you about to make fucking room! I'm home now!" She pushed her way inside. "Where's my boy?"

COMING SOON

The House That Crack Built 2

Russo & Amina

By KIM MEDINA

The Cartel Publications Order Form

www.thecartelpublications.com

Inmates **ONLY** receive novels for $10.00 per book.
(Mail Order **MUST** come from inmate directly to receive discount)

Shyt List 1	_____	$15.00
Shyt List 2	_____	$15.00
Shyt List 3	_____	$15.00
Shyt List 4	_____	$15.00
Shyt List 5	_____	$15.00
Pitbulls In A Skirt	_____	$15.00
Pitbulls In A Skirt 2	_____	$15.00
Pitbulls In A Skirt 3	_____	$15.00
Pitbulls In A Skirt 4	_____	$15.00
Pitbulls In A Skirt 5	_____	$15.00
Victoria's Secret	_____	$15.00
Poison 1	_____	$15.00
Poison 2	_____	$15.00
Hell Razor Honeys	_____	$15.00
Hell Razor Honeys 2	_____	$15.00
A Hustler's Son	_____	$15.00
A Hustler's Son 2	_____	$15.00
Black and Ugly	_____	$15.00
Black and Ugly As Ever	_____	$15.00
Year Of The Crackmom	_____	$15.00
Deadheads	_____	$15.00
The Face That Launched A	_____	$15.00
Thousand Bullets		
The Unusual Suspects	_____	$15.00
Miss Wayne & The Queens of DC	_____	$15.00
Paid In Blood (eBook Only)	_____	$15.00
Raunchy	_____	$15.00
Raunchy 2	_____	$15.00
Raunchy 3	_____	$15.00
Mad Maxxx	_____	$15.00
Quita's Dayscare Center	_____	$15.00
Quita's Dayscare Center 2	_____	$15.00
Pretty Kings	_____	$15.00
Pretty Kings 2	_____	$15.00
Pretty Kings 3	_____	$15.00
Pretty Kings 4	_____	$15.00
Silence Of The Nine	_____	$15.00
Silence Of The Nine 2	_____	$15.00
Prison Throne	_____	$15.00
Drunk & Hot Girls	_____	$15.00
Hersband Material	_____	$15.00
The End: How To Write A	_____	$15.00
Bestselling Novel In 30 Days (Non-Fiction Guide)		
Upscale Kittens	_____	$15.00
Wake & Bake Boys	_____	$15.00
Young & Dumb	_____	$15.00
Young & Dumb 2:	_____	$15.00
Tranny 911	_____	$15.00
Tranny 911: Dixie's Rise	_____	$15.00

First Comes Love, Then Comes Murder _____		$15.00
Luxury Tax	_____	$15.00
The Lying King	_____	$15.00
Crazy Kind Of Love	_____	$15.00
And They Call Me God	_____	$15.00
The Ungrateful Bastards	_____	$15.00
Lipstick Dom	_____	$15.00
A School of Dolls	_____	$15.00
Hoetic Justice	_____	$15.00
KALI: Raunchy Relived	_____	$15.00
Skeezers	_____	$15.00
You Kissed Me, Now I Own You	_____	$15.00
Nefarious	_____	$15.00
Redbone 3: The Rise of The Fold	_____	$15.00
The Fold	_____	$15.00
Clown Niggas	_____	$15.00
The One You Shouldn't Trust	_____	$15.00
The WHORE The Wind		
Blew My Way	_____	$15.00
She Brings The Worst Kind	_____	$15.00
The House That Crack Built	_____	$15.00

(**Redbone 1** & **2** are **NOT** Cartel Publications novels and if **ordered** the cost is **FULL** price of $15.00 **each**. **No Exceptions**.)

Please add $5.00 **PER BOOK** for shipping and handling.

The Cartel Publications * P.O. BOX 486 OWINGS MILLS MD 21117

Name: _____

Address: _____

City/State: _____

Contact/Email: _____

Please allow 5-7 BUSINESS days before shipping.

The Cartel Publications is NOT responsible for Prison Orders rejected, NO RETURNS and NO REFUNDS.

NO PERSONAL CHECKS ACCEPTED

STAMPS NO LONGER ACCEPTED

By KIM MEDINA